the difference between
SOMEBODY and
SOMEONE

THE DIFFERENCE TRILOGY BOOK 1

USA TODAY BESTSELLING AUTHOR
ALY MARTINEZ

The Difference Between Somebody and Someone
Copyright © 2022 Aly Martinez

All rights reserved. No part of this novel may be reproduced, distributed, or transmitted without written permission from the author except for the use of brief quotations in a book review. This ebook is licensed for your personal enjoyment only. If you would like to share this book with others please purchase a copy for each person. This eBook may not be re-sold or given away to other people.

The Difference Between Somebody and Someone is a work of fiction. All names, characters, places, and occurrences are the product of the author's imagination. Any resemblance to any persons, living or dead, events, or locations is purely coincidental.

Cover Photo: Wander Aguiar
Cover Design: Hang Le
Editing: Mickey Reed
Proofreading: Julie Deaton and Julia Griffis
Formatting: Champagne Book Design

To Tom and Pat:
You have officially read more of my books
than my own parents.
Keep that up!

the difference between
SOMEBODY and
SOMEONE

chapter ONE

Bowen

THE WORLD OWES YOU NOTHING.

There, I said it. And I hope to God you actually listened because it's the best piece of advice you will ever receive. It took over thirty years of my life, five days of surviving the unimaginable, losing the woman I loved—not once, but twice—and then facing the horrific, paralyzing, and utterly impossible task of moving on without her before I finally figured it out.

The world owes you nothing. Not even a final goodbye.

When I proposed, I imagined we'd grow old together. If my mother's side of the family was any indication, my rich brown hair would have fallen out while hers would have faded into a timeless silver. We would have held hands, rocking on a porch swing while a ball of fur roughly the size of a football played fetch with our grandkids. One night we'd go to bed, she'd curl into my side, whisper I love you, and then we'd drift off into the afterlife together.

I mean, not that I'd planned our deaths or anything, but we all had romanticized thoughts on how we'd go.

This was never how it was supposed to end. Though not many things in the storm of our relationship had gone as planned.

The world owes you nothing.

It had given us even less.

To adequately convey my journey through hell, I'll need to start at the end.

The *very* end.

The last time I saw my Sally.

"Are you just going to sit there and mope the whole flight?" she snipped.

I gritted my teeth and tried—unsuccessfully—to cross my legs in the suffocating confines of the middle seat. I was six-foot-four to her five-foot-nothing, yet she had settled into the one on the aisle as soon as we'd found our seats.

Such was life with Sally.

After a muttered apology for bumping the snoring man on my other side, I flicked my gaze to the Bloody Mary in her hand. "Sorry, is my mood killing your buzz?"

Her blue eyes sparkled in the glow of the reading light. "It really is."

I shook my head and went back to mindlessly flipping the pages of a magazine I'd bought at the terminal back in Colorado. I'd picked it up with hopes it would be a distraction from the cyclone raging within me on our way back to Atlanta. The minute she ordered that drink, I'd known it was a lost cause.

Her hand came across the armrest and landed on my thigh. "Bowen, stop. It's not a big deal."

It was the truth. Compared to everything we'd been through, our house could have been swallowed by a sinkhole and it wouldn't have been considered a *big* deal.

Honest to God, I was lucky to still have her at all. It had only been nine months since we'd met, but we'd lived a thousand lives in that time. Unfortunately, that also meant we'd died almost as many deaths.

Terrifying, tortuous, agony-filled deaths.

We'd also found love though—immeasurable amounts of it.

I stared down at her engagement ring. I'd cashed out a huge chunk of my savings account and still had to open a line of credit with the jewelry store to buy the three-karat princess-cut ring. The payment was roughly the same as I paid for my truck each month, but the tears in her eyes as she'd sat in her hospital bed, clutching it to her chest the day I proposed, made it all worth it.

She was worth it. Every day, every tear, every worry-filled minute shaved off my life.

I'd do it all again.

If only I weren't so fucking helpless to save her. I loved that woman. Whole heart. Whole soul. Bend me, break me, crack me open and she would have been there. No matter how bad it got, she was always a part of me.

I wasn't sure anymore if she could say the same.

"Bowen," she whispered, just as she'd done so many times before. It was a plea. One she knew I'd answer no matter the situation. No matter how mad I got. No matter how much I feared losing her again.

My gaze instinctively lifted to hers.

She smiled and the sight caused an ache in my chest. It was a lie.

Fuck. I missed her smile.

"Baby, I'm okay." She tilted her head to her drink. "I hate flying. That's all this is."

That was a lie too.

My shoulders fell and a loud breath tore from my burning lungs, but I let myself pretend, my mind going back to a time when it could have been the truth.

I thought of the nights we'd shared multiple bottles of wine and made love, laughing and moaning under the covers until the sun crept across the horizon. She'd rested peacefully in my arms. No nightmares. No crying in her sleep. No insomnia. Just even breaths, her head on my shoulder, and her body wound around mine so tightly it was like a second skin.

But that was the past.

The unreachable, insurmountable past.

The plane jerked, forcing me back to the present.

"Shit." She moved her hand off my thigh to grasp her drink as it sloshed all over her. "Crap, crap, crap," she chanted, using a cocktail napkin to dry the dark-red pool of tomato juice on her white pants.

For a moment, I sat there and watched her struggle. It wasn't the most chivalrous thing to do, but I was all out of grand gestures.

She unbuckled her seat belt and lurched to her feet, her phone along with a handful of ice cubes from her lap falling to the floor. "Damn, this is going to leave a huge stain."

The plane jerked again and she stumbled forward, crashing into the seat in front of her before I could catch her arm.

"Dammit, sit down before you get hurt."

Ignoring me, she bent over to fish her phone from under the seat. "Hit the button for the flight attendant. I need some club soda and a lemon. STAT."

"No, what you need is to *sit down*."

I gave her arm a tug and dragged her down to the seat. Using the tip of my boot, I swept her phone toward her. Aforementioned lack of chivalry aside, I was no contortionist; leaning over to pick it up was out of the question.

She folded her upper body over my lap and blindly patted around the floor. I fought the urge to run my fingers through the back of her hair. In the beginning, it would have been a no-brainer. I'd have curled forward and suggestively whispered in her ear, "Since you're already down there…"

She would have grinned up at me, her whole face filled with mischief as she traced a finger over my zipper, ignoring anyone who dared to watch her as she replied, "You mean down here?"

I'd have grabbed her hand and made her stop even though I was the one who had started it. Sally had no filter. She always took it one step too far. I'd loved that about her when we'd first met. It was fresh and exciting, a far cry from the stuffy women I'd dated in the past.

But now, she was in the past too.

We were in the past.

Although, it wasn't fair to say she was the only one who had changed. I was a different person too. The trauma of thinking you'd lost your soul mate would do that to a man.

I worried about her. Not more than I should, but probably

more than was healthy. My sister had nagged me for months to talk to someone, but I'd felt like such a hypocrite, rushing off to therapists and doctors while she sat at home, playing with our dogs and testing out new recipes.

Still, one of us had to get help. Someone had to be the better half in this relationship. Currently, we were just two people—broken and even more broken.

And in love.

Irrevocably.

And terrified.

Constantly.

My stomach churned as I thought about what would happen after we got home. She'd go back to smiling all the time and touching me every chance she got. Then one day, I'd wake up and she'd already be awake. At first, I wouldn't be sure if it was because she'd gotten up early or if she'd never gone to sleep. As the days passed, the answers would become clear while she slowly faded into a hollow pit of nothingness right in front of my eyes.

She'd insist she was fine.

I'd have a nervous breakdown waiting for her to fall apart.

And then, two months later, we'd be right back on this plane, headed to the very same post-traumatic stress treatment facility she'd left way too soon.

It wasn't her fault. None of it.

Unfortunately, I'd learned over the last few months that my feelings of helplessness often manifested in frustration. I wanted to help her. I wanted to fix us. But all I could do was sit in the middle seat beside her, a mere passenger on her journey.

The flight attendant arrived with a stack of napkins and

a trash bag. I watched, numb and emotionless, as they joked about the pilot owing her a new drink.

There was a whole chaotic process of the flight attendant retrieving a bottle of club soda, then a lemon, then a woman behind us piping up to say lime actually worked best. The man in front of us teased that we were close to a fruit salad. Then the male flight attendant came over with a towel and informed us that if we added a little gin to all that soda and lime, we might forget about the pants altogether.

They chatted and laughed and carried on like everything was so damn normal.

It wasn't though.

They had no clue that beneath those beautiful eyes and bright smile was a fucking tragedy.

And there was not one damn thing I could do to make it better—for either of us.

The plane shook again and this time it was accompanied by a stomach dip. The pilot was on the overhead speaker in the next beat, informing us that we were beginning our descent into Atlanta and the rest of the ride might be bumpy. Equal parts relief and dread washed over me.

We were almost home.

Fuck, we were almost home.

Leaning my head back, I closed my eyes. I couldn't do this. I couldn't watch her fake it anymore.

Yet, I would.

Day after day.

Until I took my final breath. Because not having her in my life wasn't an option. It would suck. It would hurt. It would shatter me. But I'd do it. I would fucking be there for her.

At least, that had been my mindset before I realized the world owed me nothing.

There had been so many times over the last few months when I'd told myself we were at rock bottom. Things couldn't possibly get worse. However, being engulfed by the flames of hell once didn't mean you were exempt from them in the future. The odds of lightning striking the same place twice were so small it should have been an impossibility. But it must have happened at least once for there to have been odds at all.

As I listened to Sally clicking her seat belt and the flight attendant collecting trash up and down the aisle, I was oblivious that it was about to happen again.

If I'd known—if only I'd fucking known.

I would have grabbed her face and told her that, despite everything we'd been through, loving her was the single best thing I'd ever done in my life.

I would have dropped to my knees and begged for her forgiveness for not having been more patient when she'd needed me.

I would have kissed her and made sure she knew that, no matter what happened, there would never be a day when I didn't love her with my whole heart.

I would have pulled her into my arms. I would have made sure she wasn't scared. I would have made sure my Sally went out of this world cocooned in the very same unconditional love she'd always offered me.

We weren't a hundred years old after having spent the better part of a century together. We didn't have kids, much less grandkids. There was no porch swing. There was no crawling into bed together before whispered I-love-yous. But dammit, if I had only known it was the end, I'd have gone with her. Wherever it was, whatever that looked like. I just wanted to be with *her*.

However, I didn't know.

So, when she leaned in close, the scent of alcohol ghosting over my cheek as she murmured, "Come on, Bowen. I know you didn't fall asleep that fast," I pushed her away.

I didn't even open my fucking eyes to steal one last glance.

"Leave me the fuck alone, Sally."

Yeah. That was what I said to her. The very last words I said to the woman I loved more than my own life were "Leave me the fuck alone, Sally."

And hers to me?

She sighed, kissed my cheek, anchored her hand to my thigh, and mumbled, "Right. Love you too, jerk."

The world owes you nothing.

I knew this because, not ten minutes later, it stole my entire life.

chapter
TWO

Bowen

MY HANDS RESTED MOTIONLESS ON THE KEYBOARD, A spreadsheet open, but my eyes were aimed at my desk. Staring without seeing, I'd been sitting there for hours. A million thoughts swirled in my head, crashing and colliding, ricocheting off each other. I was too numb to make sense of anything.

It was all so fucking empty.

My life. My chest. My ability to put one foot in front of the other without feeling like I was going to buckle under the pressure of it all.

But there I was at work, wearing my best façade to hide the agony, when all I really wanted was to disappear.

"Bowen?" Emily, my new secretary, called over the intercom.

I startled, straightening my tie before clearing my throat to reply, "Yeah. What's up?"

"Your mom is on line one."

No surprise there. It was a miracle I'd almost made it all the way to noon without her blowing up my phone.

Sighing, I scrubbed a hand over my beard. I'd been growing the damn thing for over a month, but after thirty-two years of sporting the smooth-as-a-baby's-butt look, it still felt foreign. Truthfully, I hated it, but I'd desperately needed a change. Something, anything to make the outside feel as different as the inside.

Sally would have hated it too.

I screwed my eyes shut and let out a loud groan.

Leave me alone, Sally.

Just thinking of her sliced me to the core. It had been six months since the plane crash, yet the searing pain made it feel like only yesterday that I'd lost her. It never changed or disappeared. It hadn't even faded with time the way everyone swore it would.

Day in. Day out. It just fucking hurt.

To an extent, I'd gotten used to living with the pain. However, on days like that one, it was impossible to ignore.

I picked up the phone and hit the blinking light. "Hey, Mom."

"Hey," she breathed. "How ya doing, sweetie?"

I rocked back in my chair and stared up at the ceiling. "I'm good."

"That bad, huh?"

"I said I was good."

"Yeah, but you lie, so I assume the opposite of whatever you say."

"Fine. I'm terrible then."

"I knew it! Dammit. I told your dad I should go with you today."

I chuckled, and because it was my mom, it was almost real. "No. You shouldn't. I don't want this to be a big production." It was a huge fucking production, but downplaying the severity of my broken heart was something of a full-time job for me. "I'm going to sneak in, sit in the back, and sign whatever my lawyer needs me to sign. Then I'll go home to chug a bottle of Jack and throw the ball for Clyde and Sugar until my arm falls off or one of us passes out. Whichever comes first."

"Hmm, perhaps you could do it *sans* the Jack?"

"Mom, the Jack is the best part. That would be like me asking you not to cuss at Dad while you're cleaning the ink from the dryer after another busted pen." An oddly regular occurrence in my parents' house since my dad was the old-fashioned kind of guy who wore a pen in his shirt pocket at all times.

"That son of a bitch," she muttered under her breath. "One more time and he's out. I swear this time."

I barked a laugh. That time, it was completely genuine.

My parents were funny. The quirky type who loved each other hopelessly but also loved to give each other absolute hell. I guessed that was what you got after thirty-nine years of marriage.

They had what I'd always wanted: someone who could give me endless amounts of shit and laugh hysterically when I gave it right back. And for a while there, it was what I'd found.

Then it was what I'd lost.

I spoke around the ever-present lump in my throat. "I'm fine. Really."

"Sure. Sure. Right. Right." Translation: You're a lying sack of shit. But since today is going to be rough, I'm not going to call you on it."

Pity aside, I was grateful for the out.

I flicked my gaze to the mile-high stack of folders on the corner of my desk. As soon as the weight of my grief had lifted enough for me to leave the house again, I'd thrown myself into my job and started my own accounting firm. Taking on too many clients. Working long into the night. Anything to avoid the memories lurking in the darkness at home.

"I should probably get back to work."

"Oh hush, you own the place. Emily can take over punching 'two plus two equals four' on the calculator while you talk to your poor, neglected mother."

Oh, yes. Two plus two equals four is exactly what my mother thought I did for a living. Until tax season. Then I quickly became her favorite child.

I rolled my eyes. "Neglected? What happened? Did Tyson finally learn to do his own laundry?"

"Come on now. Don't be ridiculous."

"Mom, he's twenty-nine. I think he can manage separating the darks from the lights."

"What, and ruin his manicure? Puh-lease."

Leaning back in my chair, I stretched my legs out in front of me. "You know one of these days, he's going to get married and his husband will hate you for babying him all these years."

"Blasphemy. His wedding will be something of a passing-of-the-torch ceremony. Besides, we all know Jared adores me."

"Yes, but… Wait. Jared? Did they get back together?"

There was a quiet squeak and then the line went silent for several beats.

"Mom?"

"I, uh…don't think I was supposed to mention that."

Of course she wasn't. My whole family had been walking on eggshells with me since the accident, and as much as I appreciated it most of the time, I really fucking resented how, with something as big as my brother getting back together with his fiancé, I wasn't the first damn person he called. Hell, I'd set the two of them up. Surely that had to give me some kind of priority status on the family phone chain.

"When did this happen?"

"Oh, honey, I'm sorry. We shouldn't be talking about this. You have a lot going on today."

"Too late. You can't drop a bomb like that then expect to—"

Further conversation died when the door to my office swung open and my sister came strutting in, her designer purse swaying on her arm.

"What the fuck?" I mumbled as she made her way around the desk. Her overpowering perfume filled the room as though a path of flowers had formed in her wake.

As an outsider looking in, an x-ray of the Michaels family would look something like this:

Cassidy Michaels-Harrington: Oldest child, snob, interior designer, mother of two hellions I loved dearly, and married to an attorney who, if possible, was an even bigger snob.

Tyson Michaels: The baby, snob, finishing the last year of his plastic surgery residency and apparently re-engaged to an orthopedic surgeon who was not a snob, but in a lot of ways, he was by association because he put up with, and often encouraged, my brother's behavior.

And then there was me, Bowen Michaels: blissfully normal

accountant, stuck in the middle, wondering how in the hell my cool-ass parents had given birth to me and the co-mayors of Snobville.

They weren't all bad though. Surprisingly, despite our differences, I was close with my siblings. I wasn't sure I would have survived losing Sally if it hadn't been for Cassidy dropping everything to move in with me for the first month. And then there was Tyson, who had spent countless nights sitting on the bathroom floor beside me as gut-wrenching sobs tore from my soul.

Nevertheless, we were different people. But we were family, and I was more grateful than words could ever express that I still had them.

Just not today.

I shot to my feet. "What the hell are you doing here?"

Cassidy curled her lip. "Good to see you too, little brother."

"Is that Cassie?" Mom asked brightly. "Tell her she's late."

Fantastic. They were plotting against me. I really shouldn't have been shocked anymore, but somehow, I still was.

The base of the phone slid across the desk behind me, knocking off a cup of pens as I prowled toward her. "Tell her yourself. She's headed to your house now."

Cassidy scoffed. "No, I'm not."

"Yes, you are. You are not coming with me today. I already told all of you—*repeatedly*—I want to do this on my own."

She lifted a shoulder in a half shrug. "Well, we disagree."

"It's not up for debate," I snapped. "Jesus Christ. What is wrong with you people? I haven't been able to breathe since I woke up this morning. You think I want an audience for this? I want to go, get it over with, go home, and fucking *forget*."

With a flick of her wrist, she swept her rich chestnut hair

off her shoulder. It was one hundred percent my father's color, which he had passed down to all of us, but hair aside, she was an exact replica of my mom. Tall and lean. Green eyes. High cheekbones. A bitchy attitude that she reserved just for me. And sometimes Tyson.

"I'm not here to be your audience, Bowen. You're my brother, and I love you. I don't even have to go inside. I'll sit in the car. Whatever." She rested her hand on my arm. "And before you start pounding your chest like a caveman, think about this. *She* wouldn't want you to be alone, either."

I winced. No. *She* wouldn't have wanted any of this. But the minute that plane hit the runway, we all lost our choices in the matter.

She gave my bicep a squeeze. "Get your shit together. Let me take you to lunch, and then let's go fight for justice for all one hundred and fifty-two people who died on that flight. But most of all, for *Sally*."

My stomach sank. God, what a damn clusterfuck.

I didn't want justice. I wanted her back.

Instead, I had to go to the courthouse and listen to an attorney for Sky High Airways claim that the crash of flight 672—which killed over three-quarters of the passengers as it skidded off the runway, broke in half, and then flipped before an engine exploded—wasn't their fault.

Mechanical records said otherwise.

The aviation accident investigators said otherwise.

And the fact that I crawled into bed alone every night said otherwise too.

But, as much as I was going to hate being present at the hearing, Cassidy was right. With only twenty-seven survivors, something had to be done. A multimillion-dollar class action lawsuit wasn't exactly what I would call justice. The alternative was allowing a billion-dollar company to walk away from the death of one hundred and fifty-two souls with little more than a six-figure fine from the Federal Aviation Administration.

The majority of the victims' families settled out of court, but the survivors had banded together in multi-district litigation that was ultimately consolidated into one court. Short of signing my name on the paperwork, I'd avoided everything to do with the damn lawsuit. But today, Sky High had rushed a settlement to finally get their name out of the press, and for the first time since this nightmare had started, we were all asked to be in attendance.

I'd spent every day of the last week dreading it, talking myself out of it, and ultimately resigning myself to a world of pain.

I didn't need reminders of that day. I'd never forget it.

Not rousing to consciousness, confused and panic-stricken in the middle of fiery wreckage.

Not the ear-piercing screams of people begging for help or the heart-stopping silence of the bodies strewn across the runway.

Not finding her lifeless and covered in so much blood that she was barely recognizable.

Not the way her ribs crunched as I endlessly performed CPR with a broken arm and punctured lung.

Not when they dragged me off her.

Not when I screamed her name until I began to choke on the smoke.

Not even the hell-spun reality of when I found out Sally had never truly left the carnage on that runway, which all but guaranteed I'd be stuck in that purgatory for the rest of my life too.

No. I didn't need reminders at all.

But as I stared at my sister while holding a phone with my meddling mother on the other end of the line, I was more pissed that I actually needed her and less so about how they'd sprung it on me at the last minute.

I was sick and fucking tired of my family feeling like they had to check in on me at every turn to make sure I wasn't on the verge of self-destruction. And worse, I was sick of them being right.

But today was the end.

In a few hours, everything would be over. The fight. The lawsuit. The never-ending roar of what-ifs playing in the back of my mind.

Surrendering, I seethed, "Fine. But you're sitting in the car *and* paying for lunch."

Cassidy's face split with a wicked grin. "I accept those terms."

My mom blew out a relieved breath over the phone. "Oh, thank God."

Pinching the bridge of my nose, I closed my eyes and rumbled at my mother, "I'm not speaking to you for a week."

"That'll make it awkward when I bring you dinner tonight, but okay, sure."

"Mom, I don't need dinner. What part of Jack, Clyde, Sugar, and throwing a ball until my arm falls off did you misunderstand?"

"Clearly the part where you take a break from destroying the perfectly good liver I provided you with in the womb and playing fetch with my granddogs to have dinner with your parents. See you at six. Kisses." She hung up.

Out-fucking-standing.

In what could only be described as the devil playing his ace in the hole, my office door once again swung open and Tyson came rushing inside. "Sorry I'm late." His chest heaved as he planted his hands on his hips. "Well, not really true. I planned to be late because I figured Cass would be late too." He narrowed his eyes on my sister. "Thanks for making me look like the ass."

She rolled her eyes. "You *are* the ass. Always and forever. This isn't new information."

They started to bicker as only the Michaels siblings could in the face of grief.

But then again, the world owed me nothing.

Not even peace and quiet as I waited for the universe to swallow me whole.

chapter
THREE

Remi

MY BARE FEET PADDED AGAINST THE HARDWOOD AS I ROUNDED the corner into the kitchen.

I blinked. Once. Twice. I threw in a third for good measure when he didn't disappear or burst into flames. "You can't be serious right now?"

He froze, a spoon halfway to his mouth. "What?"

Growling, I stomped over and snatched the box of Frosted Flakes off the table. "Dammit, Mark, stop eating my cereal. We literally just had this conversation last night."

He arched a dark eyebrow. "No. We discussed you not running ten humidifiers for your four million plants to the point I wake up confused if I'm in bed or lost in the Amazon. Then… you got mad, pouted, and ordered moo shu chicken just so you could put it in the refrigerator and tell me not to eat it. You never said anything about cereal."

The majority of it was true, though I didn't have four

million plants. I wasn't even to triple digits yet. And I only turned on nine humidifiers, so really, his argument had holes.

He shoved the spoon into his mouth, smiling as he chewed. "Relax. I'll buy you more."

"No, you won't." I gave the box a shake, hearing nothing but the dusty remnants of my favorite breakfast. "Besides, what the hell good does it do me now? I have to leave in ten minutes."

He raked his gaze over the towel pulled tight around my middle all the way up to the smaller one tied around my hair. "Then I think you have bigger problems than cereal."

In theory, living with my two best friends sounded like a dream when we'd moved in together four years earlier. We had all been bright-eyed and bushy-tailed twenty-five-year-olds with the world at our fingertips. Mark had been saving up to open his own bar while Aaron had been climbing the corporate ladder. I, on the other hand, had still been contemplating world domination. (Read: unemployed.) So, honestly, sharing a house with my two best friends and splitting the bills three ways had been a godsend for me.

Though living with two men who were allergic to grocery shopping, unloading the dishwasher, and putting the toilet seat down left a lot to be desired.

Don't get me wrong. I loved my guys. Living together was just *a lot* sometimes.

The three of us were different in virtually every way, but when we'd met in high school, those differences were exactly what we'd needed at the time.

Freshman year had started out fantastic for all of us. I was one of the popular girls. Co-captain of the cheerleading squad, known for my kindness and generosity without ever having done anything that wasn't purely self-serving. My father owned a restaurant, The Wave, which had the most incredible loaded cheese fries. And if you were with me, those cheese fries were free.

My perfect little life came crumbling down when news broke of my mom's affair with our married Spanish teacher. I didn't think anyone actually cared that my mom was sleeping with Mr. Ruiz, but nothing set a high school on fire like a scandal. For reasons I would never understand, I found myself burning at the stake over other people's choices that had absolutely nothing to do with me. My friends stopped talking to me, my parents got a divorce, and my mom and Mr. Ruiz moved to Texas. Being that I was fifteen with my world falling apart, I chose to stay in the only place I felt at home: with my dad and his free cheese fries.

Cue Aaron Lanier.

High school was the fresh start he'd been waiting for after a less-than-stellar stint in middle school. His high hopes lasted approximately twelve seconds before he was labeled as the gay kid—again. Back then, Aaron was the type of guy who never truly seemed comfortable in his own skin. It didn't help his case that he preferred khakis over basketball shorts and meticulously styled his hair every morning while the rest of the ninth-grade boys were lucky if they had showered and put on deodorant.

As I'd learned earlier that year, it didn't take much to find yourself on the wrong side of the high school gossip train. But poor, sweet Aaron might as well have been tied to the tracks. His locker had been decorated with condoms and free HIV testing fliers on the regular, and by the end of the year, he'd been locked inside so many closets that the janitorial staff had given him his own set of keys to get out. His luck should have changed when David Scott, star defensive lineman of the football team, came out in front of the entire school by asking Aaron to homecoming.

Come on. That was the stuff high school romances were made of.

One problem. Despite a million rumors that said otherwise, Aaron wasn't gay.

The words "I'm sorry, but I'm straight," had barely cleared his lips before they were echoed around the entire school, leaving brave David the victim and Aaron the ultimate villain.

All too familiar with how quickly a thousand-plus students could turn on you, I dragged Aaron out of the lunchroom, horror showing on his bright-red face. He didn't know me, but there was something to be said about having a person who understood what you were going through.

After that, the two of us became inseparable. He walked me to class every morning, ate lunch with me behind the gym every day, and did his homework with me at The Wave every afternoon. It wasn't long before the school thought we were dating. Aaron was so grateful for the confirmation of his sexuality that we never corrected the assumptions.

On the first day of junior year, Mark Friedman entered our lives and completed our misfit throuple. He was new to school, and I nearly had a heart attack when I saw all six-foot-five of him dressed in Unabomber chic, sitting in Aaron's spot behind the gym. I mean, it wasn't like we had reserved seating or anything, but after two years of wearing down the grass into a patch of dirt, we liked to think we'd staked our claim.

So I took a chance and asked the giant if he was lost.

He told me to fuck off.

I told him he didn't have to be such an asshole.

He told me to fuck off again.

Aaron jumped in and told *him* to shut the fuck up, but in true Aaron fashion, he tacked on a please at the end of it.

There was a beat where I was fearful for Aaron's life, but a wide smile split Mark's mouth. He lifted his hands in surrender, muttered an, "Easy there, killer," and then scooted over exactly six inches.

And that was how Mark joined our group.

Compared to Aaron's rich and pretentious parents and my say-anything single dad, Mark's home life was rough. His father was a drunk who never left the couch, and his mother was addicted to painkillers and rarely left the bed. They survived on turmoil, arguments, and staying off social services' radar. For a teenager with a stomach as big as his heart, Mark couldn't get by with an empty fridge and bare cupboards. But I had free fries, which my father quickly upgraded to all-you-can-eat burgers, chicken fingers, and anything else on the menu and Aaron had a guest room where Mark stayed more often than he did his own home.

After high school, we all drifted off to separate colleges. But when we came home for holidays and summer vacations, it was as if nothing had changed. I didn't even search for an apartment when I moved back to Atlanta; living with my guys was the logical choice. I'd cussed my choice in roommates under my breath more times than I could count, but I had never regretted it.

All our financial situations had changed over the years. Mark's bar, The Rusty Nail, was thriving. Aaron was computer engineering at a large company downtown, and as of recently, I had earned my brokerage license and opened my own real estate company. We could all afford our own places now, and each one would have been bigger than the eighteen-hundred-square-foot rental we shared. But there was something unbelievably comfortable about our arrangement that made us all stay.

Well, that and Mark's eternal bachelor status, Aaron's fear of commitment, and my inability to meet a man who even remotely piqued my interest.

Okay, maybe comfortable and *sad* was a better description of our living arrangement. It worked for us though.

Most of the time.

I snatched the bowl from Mark and carried it to the drawer where I dug out a spoon. Leaning against the counter, I gave him a pointed smile before shoveling a huge bite into my mouth.

Crossing his arms over his chest, he sank back into his chair and shot me a glare that held no heat. "Savage."

I shrugged, chewing as loud as I could—all too aware of how much it annoyed him.

Bite after bite, our stare off continued until Aaron suddenly ruined breakfast for both of us.

"Remi!"

I jumped, sloshing all but a few bites of the Frosted Flakes onto the floor.

Mark let out a loud laugh.

I leveled my glare on Aaron. "What the hell? Why are you yelling?"

He put his hand in the air and mimicked strangling me, his navy blazer opening to reveal a tailored vest beneath it. "Better question: What the hell are you still doing in a towel?"

I looked at the mess on the floor. "Well, I *was* eating. Now, it looks like I'm cleaning."

"We don't have time for this." He marched over, carefully avoiding the milk puddle that would have made Tony the Tiger cry. After snagging the bowl from my hands, he unceremoniously dropped it into the sink. "We have to leave in five minutes, and you aren't even dressed yet. We can't be late today, Remi." He let out a huff and started to brush his blond hair off his forehead before remembering that his unruly locks were already sealed in place with a rather obnoxious amount of gel. Instead, he pinched the bridge of his nose. "We just…can't."

Mark and I exchanged knowing glances.

Six months earlier, Aaron and I had been on a flight home from Colorado when, due to improper balance and faulty landing gear that never should have been approved for takeoff, our plane broke apart upon landing. Twenty-seven people survived, but even without physical scars, no one was immune to the catastrophic trauma of a disaster like the one we'd experienced.

Aaron was no longer the soft-spoken kid who had been bullied in high school. He was over six feet tall, and four mornings a week, he could be found at the gym with Mark. Women stopped dead in their tracks on the sidewalk when he passed, and there wasn't a woman at his office who didn't openly gape at him. He was one of the strongest men I'd ever met, but since the accident, he'd been struggling.

He had nightmares—a lot.

Anxiety that crept up on him from out of nowhere.

And sometimes, he just got overwhelmed with life in general.

I shifted my gaze to Mark and all humor over our breakfast exchange vanished.

Standing from his chair, he locked his gaze on our best friend. "You hanging in there, man?"

Aaron rubbed his eyes with his thumb and forefinger. "We don't have time for this. You know how I hate being late."

I frowned. The man did have a thing for punctuality, but it wasn't why he was toeing the line of a panic attack.

My stomach became tight as I watched him chew on his bottom lip. There was nothing I wouldn't have done to take that away from him. But no two people on the plane had had the same experience. The minute those wheels hit the ground, our lives were ripped apart. We came home to the same house. Slept in rooms that were across the hall. Quietly ate breakfast at the same table each morning. But just like the cabin of that plane, something had been broken.

God bless Mark. I had no idea what the two of us would have done without him. As much as Aaron and I tried to be there for each other, broken couldn't fix broken.

Mark never knew the right thing to say or do, but he tried. If I woke up confused or afraid, he was the first one in my bedroom, arms open wide. And when it was Aaron's turn to lose it, Mark would sit for hours at the foot of his bed, talking him down.

It was memories like those that made me feel guilty for not letting him eat my Frosted Flakes. He deserved the whole damn cereal aisle.

Mark loomed over us, flicking his gaze between Aaron and me. "You want me to go with you guys? I can have Eric meet the beer distributer at the bar. It won't take me but a minute to get dressed."

"No," Aaron returned immediately. "It's fine. I'm fine. We're all just fucking fine."

I gave his arm a squeeze, letting it linger. "I'll be ready in five. I promise."

His face softened and his shoulders rolled forward. "I'm sorry. I…"

I shook my head. "Hey, you don't have to explain anything. Let me go get dressed. You drive, and I'll do my makeup on the way. Okay?"

He nodded and offered me a tight smile. "Okay."

On my way out of the kitchen, I bumped my shoulder with Mark's. At five-two, I barely came up to his chest, so realistically, it was more like bumping my shoulder with his elbow.

He shot me a wink and slanted his head toward my room. *Go. I got this*, he silently replied.

My chest warmed. Comfortable and sad aside, this was why we were all twenty-nine, successful, and still living together.

Just before I got to my room, I barked a laugh when I heard Mark start in on Aaron.

Remember the aforementioned part about him never knowing what to say or do? Proof: "So, Mr. Three-Piece Suit, did you prepare a speech to accept your Oscar or are you just going to wing it?"

"Shut the fuck up," Aaron bit back, but there was no mistaking the humor in his tone.

chapter FOUR

Remi

I SHOULD HAVE KNOWN BETTER THAN TO WEAR THAT DAMN BLACK MAXI dress. I didn't personally believe in witches or magic, but it was cursed. There was no other explanation for it. I'd survived two of the worst dates of my life in that dress and broken a heel while on my way to show a million-dollar home in that dress. It was also what I'd been wearing the day I found out a buyer had been arrested on embezzlement charges an hour before the biggest closing of my life.

So when I said the dress contained some seriously bad vibes, I was not exaggerating.

I had no idea why I hadn't burned the damn thing yet, but after I'd promised Aaron I'd be ready in five minutes, it turned out to be my saving grace. Banished to the dark depths of my closet, it was in the bag from the dry cleaners when I found it. Since it was the only article of clothing I owned that didn't need to be ironed, I took a chance.

Now, I was paying the price.

On the car ride over, I twisted my unruly blond hair into a loose braid that hung over one shoulder, and despite the potholes, which I swear Aaron hit on purpose, my makeup was *almost* perfect. For as much as I'd been dreading the day, I felt pretty good when we walked up to the courthouse. There was a line down the front steps to get through security, so Aaron and I made small talk while we waited. The usual stuff: work, the bills, the brunette in front of us who was one hair flip away from breaking her neck to catch his attention.

And that was when the black maxi dress from hell got its ultimate revenge for being awakened from its peaceful, plastic-wrapped slumber.

I thought nothing of the little string when I saw it flapping in the breeze. At first glance, it didn't look like it was attached to the dress at all. More like a loose fiber that had landed there by chance.

Oh, how wrong I was.

That bastard string slid out without so much as an argument. And with it, the whole left side of my top fell open like Janet Jackson at the Super Bowl halftime show.

Aaron scrambled, trying to block me from view, but there were a solid ten people who got up close and personal with my bra.

Fortunately, I had a wonky-looking safety pin at the bottom of my purse that Aaron and I managed to rig the traitorous dress back into place with just before we reached the metal detector.

Unfortunately, I'd forgotten to take the pepper spray out of my purse, so we were turned away, but being that he was my best friend and possibly still scarred for life after being so close to my boob, Aaron agreed to run my accidental contraband back to the car so I didn't have to throw it away. Then, because the black maxi dress from hell wasn't done with its reign of terror yet, he'd barely disappeared around the corner when the safety pin gave up on life and popped off my dress.

Ten more scandalized people and a seventy-something security guard who shot me a wink later, there I was—on my knees, holding my dress to my chest with one hand and using two twigs I'd broken off a shrub to dig the pin out of a crack in the steps like a game of Operation. It was a worthless effort. The damn pin might as well have entered the witness protection program, never to see the light of day again.

Okay. Plan B. When Aaron got back, I'd ask him for his suit coat. I'd have to button it closed and I'd look absolutely ridiculous, but at least we wouldn't be late.

Careful not to give the dwindling line of spectators another show, I crisscrossed my arms over my chest and stood to my full height. My one remaining strap slipped off my shoulder and I swung my elbow up to keep it from falling down my arm.

Business as usual in the cursed dress from hell.

Except for the fact that pain exploded in my elbow.

"Ow!" I exclaimed at the same time I heard someone rumble, "Shit."

Grabbing my elbow, I spun and found a man on the stair below me using both hands to cover his nose. And because I needed to seriously work on respecting personal boundaries, I lurched toward him, stacking a hand over his as if three hands covering his injury were the medically recommended amount.

"Oh, God, I'm so sorry."

"Son of a…" he trailed off when he opened his eyes.

Holy shit. The most gorgeous golden-brown eyes I'd ever seen collided with mine. And I don't mean that our eyes simply met. I mean, they met and locked and I somehow ended up pregnant in the span of one blink.

Fantastic. He was gorgeous, and I'd potentially broken his nose, wrecking a perfect profile.

"Are you okay?" I asked. He was tall, but I was on the step above him, so we were almost level and only inches apart—the perfect missionary position for a mutual eye-fuck. Except, based on his furrowed brows, this was a solo act.

"Shit," he repeated, clearing his throat and backing down a step, out of my reach. As he lowered his hands, my breath caught. He had full lips, and even hidden beneath a closely trimmed beard, I could make out a sharp jawline. His nose though…

"You're bleeding."

"What?" He immediately rubbed above his upper lip, effectively spreading the small drop of crimson across his cheek.

I squeaked and bit my bottom lip. "You, uh, smeared it. Hold on. I think I have a tissue—" The words died on my tongue when Mr. Tall, Dark, and Handsome reached into his front breast pocket and pulled out a handkerchief.

No, really. A *handkerchief*.

He dabbed at his nose, cursing when he saw the bright red on the clean white linen.

Unsure what the proper protocol was after accidentally assaulting a man, I opted for a round of apologies. "I'm so sorry. Are you headed inside? Maybe I can find you some ice?" I twisted my lips and glanced around, wondering if my security guard admirer had access to a break room.

"I'm fine," he grumbled. "Jesus." He diverted his gaze over my shoulder. "Your dress...broke."

I grabbed the forgotten strap and did the best I could to cover my chest. "For the record, you should know that this dress is haunted. You may have inadvertently touched it when I hit you, so my recommendation would be to use a generous amount of hand sanitizer and potentially a sage aura cleansing at your earliest convenience."

For several beats, he blinked at nothingness behind me, his long, dark lashes brushing his cheeks. Just when I started to worry that I might have given him a concussion, he muttered, "Sage. Right." He roughly shoved the bloodied handkerchief into his pocket before retrieving his wallet. Using one long finger, he dug around in a small pocket in the front of his brown leather bifold then extended a silver safety pin toward me. The good, sturdy kind—not like the cowardly one hiding in the cracks at our feet.

I grinned. "Well, aren't you prepared for everything. First a handkerchief, now a secret safety pin? What else are you hiding in that suit?"

Yes. I was flirting. He might have been dry, stoic, and probably completely uninterested. But he was gorgeous, appeared to be around thirty, and wasn't wearing a wedding ring. That was the trifecta of my type.

His brows drew together, but his gaze never came back to mine.

Not as he jerked his chin in a silent goodbye.

Not as he turned on a toe and took the rest of the stairs two at a time.

Not even as I yelled at his back, "Thank you! Sorry again about your nose!"

And it was a real shame because his backside was just as gorgeous as his front.

~

"Holy shit," I mumbled.

The sentiment was spoken simultaneously with Aaron's whispered, "Oh, fucking fuck."

The courtroom was packed. People crammed, shoulder to shoulder, on the long wooden benches. Huddles had formed in the aisle, and quiet conversations hummed as though we were at a library.

"Breathe," I quietly reminded him, hooking my arm through his, pressing myself into his side. I told myself I was comforting him, but uninvited nerves fluttered in my stomach as we made our way through the crowd.

"Why are there so many people here?" he asked.

"Right? Is there an open bar no one told us about?"

"Good idea. Let's go get drunk and then come back."

"Oh, no you don't." I gave his arm a tug. "We can have drinks tonight when this is over. Hopefully by then, you can buy a whole bottle of tequila on Sky High's dime."

His face got hard. "I don't want their money, Remi. And you shouldn't, either."

I narrowed my eyes. "I don't, but there's nothing wrong with celebrating the fact that they no longer have it."

He blew out a ragged breath. "Why do we have to be here?"

I opened my mouth, hoping a grand pep talk would

vocalize out of thin air, but I was interrupted before I had the chance to find out.

"Remi!"

I plastered on a smile before I turned to see a beautiful woman with a sophisticated black bob rolling our way.

Katherine Gates.

Everyone processes tragedy in a different way.

Some shut down and get lost in the emotion, spending their days fighting demons and trying to forget.

Some get angry, rage at the world, and try to find someone to blame in the hopes that it will release them from the suffocating weight of their guilt.

Some turn inward, trying to figure out why they were one of the few chosen to survive, and then they dedicate their lives to repaying Karma for sparing their life.

And some, like Katherine, create an email distro for all the survivors to share essential oil concoctions, cat memes, and plan monthly get-togethers no one attended.

"Hey, Katherine," I greeted, releasing Aaron's arm to bend down and give her a hug. "You look gorgeous today."

She beamed up at me with a bright smile. "Thanks. You too."

"Aaron, this is Katherine Gates. Katherine, this is—"

"Aaron Lanier." She extended her hand. "So nice to finally meet you. You're number twenty-six for me. Only one more and I'll have met all the survivors. What's your number?"

Shaking her hand, he chuckled uncomfortably. "Including you? Two."

"Oh, honey. Don't forget to count yourself. You're a survivor too."

He chuffed. "I don't know about all that. I'm *surviving*. I'm not sure I'm to the *survivor* part yet."

She cradled their joined hands and tugged him down. "You'll get there. We'll all get there. We just have to stick together."

"Sure," he whispered, gently freeing his hand from her grip. Lately, optimism was not Aaron's strong suit.

With narrowed eyes, she watched him for several beats, and just before the shroud of awkwardness suffocated us all, she looked at me. "How are your arms?"

She didn't mean anything by it, but guilt still slashed through me. I'd been luckier than most.

Katherine hadn't been in a wheelchair the day she'd boarded flight 672. I'd never been brave enough to ask for the specifics of her injuries, but they were extensive. In the early days of her emails, she'd updated us all from a hospital bed. Then a rehabilitation center. Recently, she'd sent photos of home renovations to accommodate her wheelchair. Her communications were always upbeat and filled with positivity, but it was times like that when I couldn't imagine how she hadn't become an erupting volcano of bitterness.

I smiled tightly. "Good as new."

"I'm glad to hear it." And she was. Genuinely. The world needed more people like Katherine Gates.

Her husband suddenly sidled up beside her, resting his hand between her shoulder blades. "Remi, it's so good to see you again."

Aaron's body jerked before he swung an accusing glare my way. "*Again?*"

Shit.

the difference between SOMEBODY and SOMEONE

Yeah, okay, fine. I'd attended a few of Katherine's get-togethers. I felt bad that no one ever went. I hadn't mentioned it to Aaron because he would have rather been shot out of a cannon into a pool of hungry sharks than attend a "survivor's mixer." But at the same time, he would have gone just so I didn't have to go alone. We had this really fun relationship where we took turns emotionally drowning for each other. It was super healthy.

I ignored his reaction. "You too, Tim. You still treating our Katie here to your culinary genius every night?"

"Torturing her with it is more like it." He leaned in and used his hand to curtain off his mouth, but he never lowered his voice. "But the dogs are getting fat off the scraps she sneaks them when she thinks I'm not looking. So I guess it's working out for them."

Katherine giggled and Tim stared down at her, pure awestruck love painting his face. If I weren't so damn relieved to know that true love did exist, I would've been jealous.

"It was good to see you, Remi. Don't be a stranger. But if you'll excuse me, I need to steal my bride away from you for—"

Hyperaware of his wife, his words faded into nothingness as her head snapped up.

"Twenty-seven," she gasped.

Aaron and I turned, following her gaze to the man walking through the double doors.

My hand came up to cover the safety pin holding up the strap on my dress as Mr. Tall, Dark, and Nice Ass walked into the room. My lips curled into a smile only seconds before my stomach dropped.

The Sky High judgment wasn't the only case happening in the courthouse that day. When I'd literally slammed into him outside, I hadn't considered why he was there. It explained his attitude though. Then again, I had elbowed-jacked him in the face. That was enough to dim even the sunniest disposition.

I watched as his long legs carried him through the crowd, but his head stayed down even as people tried to stop him.

I tapped Aaron's foot with the toe of my high heel and whispered, "That's the guy who gave me the safety pin."

"You met Bowen?" Katherine asked, clearly not giving the first damn that she had eavesdropped.

"Briefly out front. Why do you sound so surprised?" I kept my gaze locked on the navy suit stretched across his muscular frame as he backed into the corner on the far side of the room. He retrieved his phone from his back pocket, but his thumbs never touched the screen. It appeared that he was using it as more of a Do Not Disturb sign than anything else.

Katherine rolled forward to share my view of him. "Bowen Michaels is something of a mystery. Word is that when Sean Meyers reached out to him to say thank you, he didn't get much more than a chin nod before Bowen slammed the door in his face."

"Wait. Why was Sean thanking him?"

Shaking her head, she shot me a bored glare. "You'd know if you read more than the subject line of my emails."

"Hey, I...skim."

She cut me a side-eye. "Bowen saved Sean's family after the crash. They were pinned under a big piece of debris, still trapped in their seats. Bowen somehow flipped it off them. Mom, dad, two young boys. An entire generation survived because of him."

"Wow," I breathed. "That's...incredible."

"Yeah, but Bowen didn't want any part of the recognition. I'm shocked he showed up today."

I slanted my head and stared at his thankfully still-flawless profile, his jaw hard and his lips tight. Intrigued even more now than during our brief interaction. "Is he local?"

Katherine didn't have a chance to reply before Aaron gave my arm a warning yank.

"Good Lord," he said, "can we sit down already. I'm about to peel out of my skin here."

Immediately, I spun to face him. Sweat beaded his forehead.

Okay, fine. Beading was generous. Sweat *dripped* down his temples.

"Okay, okay," I soothed. "Sorry. I got distracted."

"Thank you," he rushed out, his shoulders falling with relief.

But still, even as I walked toward a thankfully open spot in the back row, I couldn't help putting my chin to my shoulder to steal one last glance at Bowen.

Less than an hour later, Sky High Airways settled to the tune of fifty-six million dollars.

It still wasn't enough.

chapter
FIVE

Bowen

One month before the plane crash…

I SMILED TO MYSELF, SETTING MY BRIEFCASE BESIDE THE TABLE NEXT TO the front door. As expected, my small three-bedroom ranch was a disaster, but that was a big part of why I was smiling. It had been too long since she'd stayed with me. I understood why—fucking hated it—but understood nonetheless. Though having her there was the only time my place ever truly felt like home.

Prominently on the coffee table, standing tall in the center of chaos, was a card with a watercolor heart painted on the front.

My chest swelled with hope that it was her reluctant agreement to go to the rehabilitation facility her doctor had suggested. The same place I'd taken out a second mortgage on my home to be able to pay for. The same place we'd fought about for hours the night before—me yelling, then apologizing. Her yelling, then crying. It was a vicious cycle for us. I'd let it go when she'd finally agreed to stay the night—small victories and all—but the conversation was far from over.

Maybe at some point during the day, she'd come around to the idea of going. Ninety days wasn't that long. I mean, it would feel like an eternity without her, but time wasn't a factor as long as she got the help she needed.

Secretly, I knew I was fooling myself, but hope had become my drug of choice.

Plucking the thick card stock off the table, I drew in a deep breath. The smell of freshly baked brownies—or cookies, or whatever-the-hell concoction of deliciousness she had been baking all day—filled my nose. For a woman who had burned grilled cheese the first time she'd cooked me dinner, she had developed a real flair for baking.

It was one of the few things she enjoyed. And let's be honest, during the ultimate battle of trying to claw our way up from rock bottom, a marshmallow-graham-cracker brownie was a nice reprieve every once in a while.

"Baby, I'm home," I called down the hall.

Like the worst guard dogs in history, Clyde and Sugar finally realized that someone else was in the house and went nuts, barking and slipping on the wood floor as they raced down the hallway. Clyde was a brindle purebred mutt while Sugar was a black teacup poodle with the temperament of a Doberman. If either of them were ever going to put up a fight, you could bet your ass it would have been Sugar. Though Clyde appeared to have some Great Dane at the deep end of his gene pool, so he'd at least look intimidating while he invited a serial killer in to play ball.

Tucking the card under my arm, I squatted down to pet them. "Hey, guys."

Oh, and yes, Sugar was a boy. Sugarbear Thadius Michaels to be exact. Sally had had quite a few drinks that night. I had just been so damn happy to see her laughing that she could have named him Princess Pineapple and I wouldn't have argued.

As I gave Clyde a scratch behind his ears, Sugar bounced off my legs, his paws leaving mud on my khaki slacks. I shouldn't have gotten frustrated, but they were new pants and I'd slept exactly three hours the night before. When it came to Sally, I was past the point of what was considered creepy anymore. Staying up and watching her sleep was my favorite pastime—my *only* pastime.

At least she was sleeping.

Breathing.

Not in pain.

Her mind was still for the first time in weeks.

"Oh, come on, Sug," I grumbled, pushing him away as I tried to brush the dirt off my pants. While I loved the hell out of that crazy dog, he was still a puppy and I shuddered to think where he had found mud in the house.

Looking back, I'd have given my entire life—past, present, and future—for it to have actually been mud. However, there was no mistaking the crimson-red blood smeared across my thigh.

My heart stopped as I frantically scooped the dog up, begging and praying to any and every god in the universe that he'd cut his paw or broken a toenail. Anything that would've made the blood his—and not hers.

See, that was what made hope a drug. After two previous

suicide attempts, combined with our fight and her overall deterioration that had led up to talks of an inpatient treatment facility to begin with, it being her blood was the most likely conclusion.

But hope clouded reality. It made me believe that anything was possible.

Like maybe she was feeling better.

Maybe I was jumping to conclusions.

Maybe the woman I was unconditionally and irrevocably in love with would stop fucking trying to die.

All hope was gone when the blood on Sugar's black fur covered my arm.

I didn't remember putting him down or dropping the card.

Nor did I remember sprinting down the hall.

I shouted her name. I was sure of it.

At some point before I reached the bedroom, I dug my phone from my pocket and dialed nine-one-one.

As much as it destroyed me, I'd mastered the process of finding her like that.

She might not have wanted to stay, but I would have done anything to keep her.

"Fuck!" I boomed as I entered the room, finding her curled into the fetal position on the bed. My bed. What I had hoped would one day be *our* bed. The white sheets were covered in blood. My every nightmare playing out in front of me—again.

And just when I thought my scarred and tortured heart was unable to break any more, pain from the explosion in my chest rocked me to the core.

A female dispatcher spoke in my ear. "Nine-one-one, what is your emergency?"

With long strides, I hurried to her side and immediately

checked for a pulse. It was faint, but a surge of adrenaline cleared the fog of fear from my head. "I need an ambulance. Fourteen-eleven Millstone Drive. My fiancée… She tried to kill herself."

There were going to be more questions. Her name. Her age. How she was injured. Where she was located in the house. How long ago it had happened. Only some of which I had answers to. None of those answers would save her.

But I could.

And no matter how much she hated me for it, I always would.

Dropping the phone, I got to work, desperate to save the other half of my soul.

"Don't you fucking do this," I snarled, more angry at the world than at her.

Popping every button, I stripped my dress shirt off and wrapped it around her wrist, tying it as tight as possible before repeating the process with my undershirt on her other arm. "You promised me!" I raged, lifting her hands over her head to hopefully slow the bleeding until help could arrive.

Her breaths were shallow, and she was a terrifying shade of gray. Ghostly. If I was being honest, she'd been a ghost of the woman I'd fallen in love with for months.

My heart rattled my ribs as it pounded at a marathon pace, but it was the soul-crushing emotion in my throat that took my knees out.

As I sank down onto the blood-covered bed beside her, a boulder of grief settled in my gut.

What if this was it?

What if she didn't survive this time?

Tears I'd long since given up on trying to control rolled

down my cheeks. "Goddamn it, you promised me. Do you hear me? You hold on because I am not done yet," I choked, barely able to get the words out. She needed to hear it, or more realistically, I desperately needed it to be true. "You are not allowed to leave me. Not like this."

The day we'd met, I'd thought it was fate. She was perfect. Her laugh. Her chaos. The levity I felt in her presence. It took approximately an hour for me to fall in love. Deep, unwavering, life-altering love. The kind that burrows into your bones and rewrites your DNA.

But maybe the only thing that had been truly fated about our relationship was the fact that I had been destined to lose her from the start.

chapter SIX

Remi

"Please tell me this is a joke," I said. My father's rickety office chair let out a loud creak as I leaned back and lifted a napkin with a handwritten IOU.

His thick gray mustache did little to hide his sheepish smirk. "What? Kenny always pays." He cut his gaze off to the side and mumbled, "Eventually."

"Which is never." I dug a manila file stuffed full of similar *paperwork* from his desk drawer. "And Allen?"

He harrumphed and rested his crossed arms on his round belly. "He's between jobs."

I paused and leveled him with a glare. "Heather?"

"Give me a break, Remi." He paced from one side of his tiny office to the other. "I don't see you complaining when I feed your boys for free anytime they show their faces around here."

"Mark and Aaron are family. Meanwhile, Heather told the entire school I had herpes after Mom left."

"You still holding grudges from well over a decade ago?" He sliced me with a disappointing scowl, making me shrink in the chair.

"Well, no... Not exactly."

"Since high school, she's had two girls and married an alcoholic who has no problem spending his rent and grocery money on booze only to come home and make her pay in different ways."

I winced, immediately feeling guilty, and my father didn't miss it.

"So yeah," he said. "Last I heard, *you* don't have herpes, but *she* does have some serious issues. If I can give her and her girls a hot meal and a safe place for a few hours, I don't give a damn if she can pay the tab or not."

God, I loved my dad. Yes, even in the middle of a grade-A scolding. He'd always had such a kind and generous heart. Perhaps not the best head for business, but he made up for it in other ways.

Resting his hand on my shoulder, he stared deep into my eyes. "Talk to me, Remi. What's really going on in that head of yours?"

Instinctively, I shrugged him off. "Nothing."

It wasn't a lie. It also wasn't the truth. I'd been off for days. I attributed it to the finality of the settlement, but putting the past to rest should have come with relief, not anxiety.

He slanted his head. "You sure? Aaron said—"

"Aaron?" I rolled my eyes. Of course they'd been talking. While he was my ride-or-die most of the time, Aaron was one hundred percent a snitch when it came to my dad. "If you want to worry about someone, your informant hasn't slept in almost a week."

"Damn," he whispered, shaking his head. "How am I supposed to leave you kids while you're still dealing with all this?"

My stomach knotted as it had so often since he'd told me he was retiring to Miami. He'd tried to cancel the move at least a dozen times after the plane crash, but if there was ever a man who deserved happiness, it was Jack Grey.

"First off, we haven't been *kids* in a long time. Secondly, I think Crystal Dawn would be pretty upset if you stood her up now."

Yes. My father married a woman named Crystal Dawn, first and middle name respectively, but he never missed an opportunity to call her by both. She wasn't a stripper. Though, if you asked me, she'd missed a pretty great opportunity with a name like that. Instead, she was a beautiful white-haired widow who carried chocolates in her purse for the neighborhood kids and thought my father had hung the moon.

I hated the idea of losing him. Not being able to swing by The Wave after a hard day and find his smiling face milling around the dining room was going to be a tough adjustment. But I had every reason to believe Crystal would take care of him.

He let out a loud groan and settled on the edge of the desk. "Come with us. I'm sure they have houses to sell in Florida. Condos too."

I lifted a handful of paper napkin IOUs in his direction. "What? And abandon all this?"

A slow smile stretched his mouth. "That was my plan."

"Then who's going to feed the Heathers and Kennys and Allens of the world?"

He finally chuckled. "Okay. Okay. Fair enough."

I had no desire to take over The Wave, but I'd grown up in the burger joint. My name was quite literally carved into the back booth, and my handprints were permanently imprinted in the sidewalk. I couldn't stand the idea of letting it close. Grey Realty kept me busy, but luckily, Mark had connections and found a full-time manager for me. Looking at the mess that was my father's bookkeeping, I probably needed a whole team.

"All right, old man. Let's get this organized before you abandon me for Margaritaville. Who's your accountant?"

"Mr. Samuel," he replied curtly.

My mouth gaped. "What the hell, Daddy? He died, like, two years ago."

"Three actually." He rose from the corner of the desk and walked toward the door. "I didn't say he was good."

"Or breathing," I smarted. "Have you been doing this on your own since then?" I pinched the bridge of my nose. "Oh, God, please tell me you've been paying taxes."

He hiked up his khaki pants. "I've been paying...some. I got a little account set aside in case they want more, but I'll be honest, the whole tax thing is a racket. If they know how much money I made, why won't they just tell me what I owe? Why do I have to figure it out on my own?"

"Oh, gee. I don't know. Maybe because it's *the law*?"

"Yeah, yeah, yeah. I'm not behind bars yet, am I?" He pulled the door open, the loud chatter of a bustling lunch rush filling the room. "I gotta get back out there. Have you eaten?"

And that was it. He was done talking. Welcome to The Wave: where paper napkin IOUs were currency and tax evasion was the house special.

"Suddenly, I'm not hungry," I replied.

"I'll make you a club sandwich for the road." The door clicked behind him.

I dropped my head to the desk. Jack Grey, with his heart of gold, was always a bit of a wildcard. Usually, I admired that about him. Now though?

I spent the next hour trying to make heads or tails of his chicken-scratch ledgers and an entire drawer of vendor receipts. True to his word, he sent one of the waitresses in with a club sandwich—no lettuce, bacon on the side, just the way I liked it—but it was a small consolation for the shitstorm he was leaving me with when he moved.

chapter
SEVEN

Remi

It was a bad idea. I knew it the moment I saw the going-out-of-business post on Facebook. However, I also knew it was a bad idea when I got in my car, drove forty-five minutes across town, and then street-parked because the parking lot was packed. None of that stopped me though.

I didn't have a lot of plants—at least not by my standards. By Mark's and Aaron's standards, my babies were just shy of being awarded rainforest protections. They swore if I brought another one home, I was going to have to move into a she-shed in the backyard, but I was *mostly* sure they were bluffing. Besides, I hadn't said anything about Mark's pilsner glass collection on the top of the kitchen cabinets or Aaron's million pairs of shoes that had taken over the hall linen closet. A few (dozen) plants were the least of their concerns.

Or so I told myself as I came face-to-leaf with the most beautiful Monstera Albo Half Moon to ever wear a clearance tag.

She was my dream plant, my unicorn, with full tropical white-and-green split leaves. While customers swirled around the shop snatching up the Pothos, African Violets, and Peperomia, she stood alone next to the cash register. This was probably because her red tag had two thousand dollars written on the back and not a buck seventy-five like everything else. But the price of variegated perfection was not for the weak of heart—or wallet.

My debit card cried a little as it was swiped, and my stomach growled with the realization that eating out would be a thing of the past for a few months, but the smile on my face never faltered. Okay, that wasn't totally true. There were quite a few cuss words uttered as I lugged the potted prize toward my car. Her leaves smacked me in the face with every step, but as I passed a small Irish pub, my obstructed gaze drifted through the windows and I came to an abrupt halt.

No way. No freaking way.

I gently slanted the ceramic pot to one side to clear my view.

Bowen—Mr. Tall, Dark, and Nice Ass himself—was sitting alone at the bar, sipping from a highball glass.

A smile immediately split my lips.

It had only been a few days since our run-in—okay, collision—at the courthouse, but I'd be lying if I didn't admit I'd thought about him in that time. I—along with the majority of the female population—was a sucker for the broody, mysterious type. Really, it was something biological and completely out of my control.

But it wasn't like we'd exchanged phone numbers or anything. What could I have done? Call Katherine, get his contact information, and show up at his front door like a crazy stalker?

Um, no, thank you. I was not that desperate. Also, Katherine didn't have his address.

I should have kept walking.

I should have left the man alone to have his drink in private.

I should have forgotten about him altogether.

Unfortunately, I'd never been good at doing what I should.

Come on. It was rather fortuitous for our paths to cross again. Twice in the same week. I could have gone to any plant shop that day. I could have parked on the other end of the street or been too hypnotized by Margret Monstera to have noticed him at all.

Who was I to deny Lady Luck?

At the very least, I could pop my head in and say hello, maybe buy him a drink as an apology for accidentally assaulting him the last time we'd seen each other. It was, after all, happy hour—he couldn't very well tell me to fuck off during such a joyous, half-price time of day.

Hitching Margret up to sit on my hip, I made my way inside with a surprisingly small number of side-eyes for a woman who was holding a three-foot-tall house plant.

"Bowen?" I said as I approached.

I couldn't see his face, but his muscular back went taut beneath his pale-blue button-down. His drink hung frozen in midair, but he made no move to look at me.

Shuffling to his side, I set Margret on the bar and then slid onto the stool beside him. "Hey, I thought that was you."

Slow and steady, he turned his head, his honey-brown gaze finding mine with an eerie calm. He said nothing as he stared at me for several beats. Clearly, the talking portion of this chance encounter was going to be left up to me—much like the last.

"I'm Remi Grey. The woman who accidentally attempted to give you a nose job outside the courthouse on Monday." I made a show of inspecting his face. "Some of my finer work, I'd say."

One blink. That was all he gave me before he became unstuck and tipped the glass to his lips. I couldn't quite tell if he recognized me and wished he didn't or if he didn't and hoped to keep it that way. But I'd already made it that far; no use in tucking tail now.

"It's so crazy running into you again. Are you waiting for someone? Girlfriend, boyfriend, worst enemy?" I internally groaned. I was terrible at this stuff. "Well, luckily, I didn't actually run into you this time, but you know what I mean."

His jaw ticked as he set his glass down, never removing his long, slender fingers from around the drink. Also never looking at me again, and short of a ragged breath which I pretended wasn't completely rude, he didn't reply, either.

Ah. The strong, silent type.

Clearly, my only course of action was to continue babbling. "What a small world, huh? I'm almost never on this side of town, but there was a plant shop having a colossal going-out-of-business sale, everything fifty to sixty percent off. Can you believe it? Who can resist a good bargain? Not this girl." I paused and swayed my head from side to side. "I guess I technically still spent more than my rent, but I got this rare beauty—and to see you again. So I'd say time and money well spent."

Much to my surprise, Bowen let out a loud cough. "More than your rent?" He peered around me. "On a weed that's half dead?"

I gasped playfully and used my hands to cover either side of a white-and-green leaf. "Shhhh, she'll hear you."

the difference between **SOMEBODY** and **SOMEONE**

His thick, dark brow shot up his forehead. "She?"

I nodded. "Margret. But all her friends call her Margie."

Shaking his head, he took another sip. "A shrub that cost as much as your rent. Jesus. Good to see the real estate business is doing well."

I was already smiling. A big, goofy, toothy, not-at-all-sexy grin. But that one statement made my mouth stretch so wide it was almost painful. Had Bowen been doing his research on me?

"And how exactly do you know I work in real estate?"

He looked away, lifting a finger for the bartender at the far end of the bar. "Grey Realty, right? Katherine might as well advertise for you in her monthly email. I've wondered if you pay her."

Two things struck me. One, Bowen reads Katherine's emails—something she would no doubt be giddy over. And two, he had not been doing any kind of research the way my obviously overinflated ego had assumed.

"Well, I don't." This wasn't going at all the way I'd hoped.

"And you certainly won't be able to now. What with all your rent thwarted for Margo's adoption."

"Mar-*gret*," I corrected.

He swiped his hands over his face and beard, blowing out an annoyed stream of air.

"Anyway," I replied, rolling my eyes at myself and buying time to come up with something that might turn the interaction around. "So, do you live around—" I began, but I was interrupted when the bartender stopped in front of us, his gaze flicking between me and Margie.

"What can I...uh, get you?"

Twisting my lips, I debated between a glass of wine or a beer, but Bowen got there first.

"Just my total."

My head swung his way. "What? Why? You haven't even finished your drink yet."

Rising from his stool, he retrieved his wallet with one hand and threw the rest of his drink back with the other.

I had to give him credit. Whatever the room-temperature amber liquid was it could not have been tasty as a shot, but he didn't make a face as it no doubt scorched his throat.

"Okay, then," I whispered to myself, the quasi-rejection scorching my throat as well.

His only reply was the sound of the empty glass landing on the bar top.

As he opened his wallet and used his thumb to slide out a credit card, a small worn imprint in the front pocket caught my attention. It didn't take but a moment for me to recognize the shape. Most men carried condoms or pictures of their families in that little pocket, yet Bowen Michaels, Man of Mystery, carried a safety pin—the very same safety pin he'd given me at the courthouse. What I found the most intriguing was that the pocket was flat. If he cared enough to carry one around with him twenty-four-seven, why hadn't he replaced it?

I didn't get the chance to ask before his wallet snapped shut. My head popped up, and I hoped he hadn't caught me staring.

Finally, luck was on my side. He was looking at the bartender. "I'll meet you down at the register."

"Sounds good." The bartender dried his hands and moseyed to the other end of the bar.

Like a gentleman, Bowen slid his stool up to the bar.

"Well, um, it was nice seeing you again," I said. "Maybe we'll run into each other again. It'd be a shame if this became a habit. Maybe next time you won't be in a hurry." Disappointed, I slouched and added, "I'll leave Margret at home. Three's a crowd."

"Have a good night, Remi," he murmured.

"You too," I told his back as he walked away without another glance.

Well, at least not another glance *from him*. I watched as he stood at the end of the bar, chatting as he paid. If I wasn't mistaken, he even smiled once at something the bartender had said. As to be expected, it was just as attractive as he was.

As his long legs carried him out the door, I succumbed to the notion that this wasn't baseball. Two strikes were more than enough for me. No wonder I liked him. Bowen Michaels, although an interesting character, wasn't interested in me.

Or so I'd thought.

A glass of white wine landed on the bar in front of me and a bottle of water slid in front of Margret.

"From the gentleman who just left," the bartender said.

I bit my bottom lip and looked over my shoulder, but Bowen was long gone.

Okay, maybe that hadn't been a strike after all. Maybe the game hadn't even started yet.

chapter EIGHT

Bowen

I DROVE HOME LIKE A MAN ON THE RUN. WHITE-KNUCKLED, MY EYES on the rearview mirror, waiting—and almost wishing—she'd suddenly appear again.

Fucking fuck me. That woman was beautiful.

If she had aimed that smile at me one more time, like a ray of Goddamn sunshine for a man sentenced to the shadows of the moon, I would have lost my mind.

Okay, not true. My mind was long gone.

"Bowen?" I could still hear her voice echoing in my head. How the fuck did she even know my name? Oh, right. Katherine, the official meddler of flight 672.

What had I done to deserve this?

Was I some kind of psychopath in a past life, reaping the punishments for my sins in the form of an intoxicating blonde with blue eyes that I swear could deliver sight to the blind?

I was not emotionally equipped to deal with Remi Grey. Christ, I was barely emotionally equipped enough to wake up each morning.

It didn't matter. It was over. Done. She was gone.

And now, I just needed to take seven thousand cold showers and then avoid McMurphy's for the rest of eternity to keep it that way.

Fan-fucking-tastic.

The house was dark when I arrived, just as it had been for the last six months, but somehow, I was still surprised by the suffocating weight of the loneliness inside. The dogs barked, the sounds of their feet on the wood floor preluding my daily welcome-home celebration. Sugar danced against my legs while Clyde took a slightly more goatly approach, head-butting me in the kneecaps.

"Okay, okay, I see you," I clipped, giving them both a placating pet before flipping the light on—and then promptly having a heart attack. "Fuck!" I boomed as my brain scrambled to make sense of why there was a man stretched out on my couch.

"It's about time you got home," my brother said, slowly sitting up.

Right. Because my day hadn't been challenging enough. "Jesus, Tyson."

He stood up, stretching his arms over his head, and yawned. "I've been waiting for over an hour. Where the hell have you been?"

Nowhere near ready to dive into that shitstorm, I avoided his question with another question. "How did you get in here?" I'd taken his key away months ago for this exact reason. If he wasn't attempting to scare the shit out of me, he wasn't truly living.

"Cassidy gave me hers when she assigned me babysitting duty tonight. Hope you're up for sushi and sake. Jared's coming to pick us up at seven."

Perfect. Just fucking perfect. Another overbearing ambush from the Michaels siblings.

"I'm going to take a hard pass on that." I walked to the kitchen, hoping and praying he hadn't eaten my leftover pizza, but if I knew him at all, the fridge had been his very first stop. "Does this mean you and Jared are officially back together?" I asked robotically, capping it off with a knowing smirk.

"Don't give me that shit. We all know Mom can't keep a secret. Telling her is cheaper than announcing it on a billboard but has the same community reach."

I laughed because he wasn't wrong. "You still should have told me." Lifting the empty pizza box off the counter, I shot him a scowl over the bar. "I hope you get food poisoning."

He grimaced. "Trust me, it felt like food poisoning going down. Who the hell puts spinach and artichoke on pizza?"

After folding the box in half, I stuffed it into the recycling bin. "Someone with tastebuds and a heathy desire to skip the gym on Sundays."

"Makes sense." He curled his biceps into a flex and kissed the molehill hiding beneath his emerald-green V-neck. "I did monopolize all the good genes in the family."

"Bullshit. Cassidy got the good genes. You got Dad's webbed toes."

"Jackass," he muttered, strolling into the small open kitchen, Sugar and Clyde hot on his heels. He propped his hip against the counter and flashed me a shit-eating grin. "Quit deflecting. I'm smarter than that. Where ya been, Bo?"

Like a truly mature adult and not at all like a ten-year-old fighting with his little brother, I curled my lip and mocked, "None of your fucking business, *Ty*."

He barked a laugh and shook his head. "You having a life isn't a crime. You know this, right?"

Retrieving a beer from the fridge, I avoided his scrutiny. "Yes. But you know what is a crime? Breaking and entering."

He snapped twice—Tyson Michaels sign language for *pass me a beer*. "Was there a woman involved in this secret after-work detour?"

I ducked back into the fridge to grab another beer, Remi and her ridiculous house plant flashing on the back of my lids.

It made no sense, her showing up at McMurphy's like that. Atlanta was a big city. Numbers were my forte, but I didn't need to break out my calculator to know the likelihood of our paths crossing was almost nonexistent.

Coincidences weren't out of the realm of possibility though.

That didn't explain why, at the courthouse, she'd stared at me like she was starving and I was her only chance at sustenance. As soon as the gavel had banged, I'd ducked out, hoping to avoid any further interactions with her. Only for an outrageously overpriced Half Moon whatever-the-fuck-she'd-called-it to hand deliver her to the barstool beside me.

There was no way I was telling Tyson—and thus my entire family—any of that.

Instead, I sliced him with a glare.

He lifted his hands in surrender. "Okay. Too soon. *Too soon.*"

I slapped a beer into his hand violently enough to make my point but not enough to potentially damage his moneymakers. With a quick flick of my wrist, I twisted the cap off and then clicked the neck of my bottle with his. "Look, I'm not up for dinner tonight. I officially dismiss you from babysitting duties. Go on a date with your boyfriend and call it a night."

He opened his beer and haphazardly tossed his cap onto the counter, earning himself another glower. "Sorry. Cass would have my balls."

"You really think she'd take them from Jared like that?"

"Hilarious," he deadpanned. "Insult me all you want, but you are stuck with me tonight. Full disclaimer, this is my first night off in two weeks, so if we are staying in, I'm making no promise about staying awake."

"You asleep and not talking to me? Don't threaten me with a good time." I took a long pull of beer.

There was no use in fighting with him. My family might as well have been surgically implanted into my ass after the plane crash. It was a wonder they hadn't started a carpool rotation to drive me to and from work every day.

"Cut me some slack. We're worried about you. First, with the settlement on Monday and now, the anniversary of..." he trailed off, shaking his head.

And just like that, it felt like a bucket of arctic water had hit me in the face. A lump formed in my throat as I looked down at my watch to check the date. With the distraction of seeing Remi again, I hadn't really considered why I'd felt the urge to go to McMurphy's that day.

I supposed, deep down, that was the answer.

Six months before the plane crash…

"I didn't mean it like that," I whispered, looking around the bar to see if anyone was watching us. I didn't care, but Sally would cower if anyone so much as glanced in her direction.

Thankfully, happy hour at McMurphy's was always slow. Their regulars didn't start pouring in until eleven, so short of a few people in the dining area, we had the place to ourselves. It was one of the selling points I'd used when convincing her to finally get out of the house for a night—something I was starting to seriously regret.

Things had been going surprisingly well for the last week. I couldn't pinpoint the why, but she seemed…happier. More at peace. The constant anxiety had ebbed into something almost resembling contentment. It was damn near euphoric watching her smile again. That was not even to mention all the times she'd kissed me or crawled into my lap, not bothering with much more than unzipping my pants before claiming what was hers.

For a whole week, we'd felt real again.

But maybe that was my biggest mistake. The tears already streaming down her cheeks were our reality now.

She leaned away from me, turning on her stool so my hand fell off her thigh. "I'm going to ask you one last time,

Bowen. And don't you dare lie to me. Not now. Not about this."

I cracked my neck, chewing on all the words I shouldn't say, but they refused to be swallowed. "I have *never* lied to you." I stabbed my finger to the other end of the bar. "Not once since we met right there three months ago."

"Then say it," she ordered.

It was the same fight we'd been having for weeks. Truthfully, it was the only fight we'd ever had, and it didn't even matter how I answered her question.

If I told her I believed her, she'd be mad I wasn't helping her search for a nameless, faceless woman who, as far as the police could tell, wasn't even missing.

If I told her I didn't believe her, with the hopes of squashing the entire conversation and getting my girlfriend back for a few hours, she'd spend every minute reliving the heartbreaking details of the terrifying ordeal that had changed both of our lives—but especially hers.

At the end of the day, this fight wasn't about whether I believed her or not. Of course, I did. Wholly and completely. The same way I loved her. This was all about me desperately trying to find the words to prevent her from once again spiraling down a never-ending hole of guilt and trauma.

I had said every combination of words in my vocabulary at least ten times, but nothing had helped. I couldn't make her understand that it wasn't her fault or responsibility. She'd survived hell and lived to tell the tale. That was something to be proud of—immensely so.

But she couldn't let it go.

Not while a woman was still out there.

Still in danger.

Still broken and scared.

So there we were, on what was supposed to be a date night after a long week, an engagement ring burning a hole in my pocket. And we were fighting over something neither of us could control.

"What do you want me to say?" I turned to face her, my hand covering hers. "Tell me what you want to hear, and I swear on my life I will say it over and over again, every day, every minute, forever, until my very last breath. And I will mean it, Sally. Every fucking word. Because while I don't have any clue what I should be saying, I know *who* I should be saying it to. I believe you. I will always believe you. I just don't know how to make you stop hurting." I brought her hand to my lips and intertwined our fingers before kissing them. "Do you remember the night we met?"

"Don't do this," she croaked, looking away, tears streaming down her cheeks.

I couldn't *not* do it. We'd only had three weeks of smiles and laughter to look back on, but those same three weeks were all it had taken to build our unbreakable foundation. The winds of life had tested us more than I had ever imagined possible, but we were still standing, the promise of a future protecting us from the storms of the present.

"You invited me back to your place to watch a movie. I could have been some kind of serial killer."

An unlikely smile curled her lips. "You ordered an appletini. Serial killers don't drink those."

Teasingly, I narrowed my eyes, so damn grateful that I'd been able to reel her in long enough for a joke. Dipping low, I rested my forehead on hers. "For the last time, I was ordering it for you. The bartender set me up."

"Whatever you need to tell yourself." Her eyes fluttered shut with a calm that made my chest ache, but her deep breath didn't contain any peace. If guilt had a sound, the soft pain-filled moan as she exhaled would have been it. "I'm sorry I'm such a mess. I don't mean to take this out on you. I just don't know what else to do."

"I know, babe," I whispered.

"She's out there somewhere and nobody is even looking for her."

I pulled her into a hug, her face fitting like a puzzle piece in the curve of my neck.

"I never even saw her face, but I can't stop imagining her alone in that room…with him." Her shoulders rolled forward with a gag. The mere mention of *him* set my blood on fire, but she didn't need my anger. "I'm just so tired. Make it stop. Please. Please, Bowen," she croaked, the weight of her frail body sagging in my arms.

I'd have given anything to do that for her. But I was failing on epic levels. For fuck's sake, I'd thought a night out and a few drinks would help.

Holding her tight with one hand, I retrieved my wallet with the other and tried not to jostle her as I threw a pile of cash onto the bar. "Let's get out of here."

The engagement ring never left my pocket that night. I hadn't wanted one of the happiest days of our lives to be tangled in pain. Though, if I was being honest, there was no way to avoid it. If something didn't give, pain was all we would ever be in together.

No. Our engagement was not the anniversary Tyson had been talking about.

Three hours after we left that bar, the love of my life tried to kill herself for the first time.

chapter
NINE

Remi

"Remi," Mark called, his large frame filling my doorway.

I snapped my laptop shut so fast it was a miracle I didn't crack the screen. "What?"

He twisted his lips, his thick, dark brows drawing together. "What are you doing? I shouted down the hall, like, three times."

Not stalking a man—that was for sure. A man who probably wasn't interested in me but had still sent me *and my plant* a drink before leaving. A man I couldn't stop thinking about. A man who, according to Google, had his own *accounting firm* when I just so happened to need an accountant for my father's paper napkin situation.

Strictly business of course.

Though said man did not have any social media accounts that I could find, thus no way to do some digging to see if he had a significant other or not. But my GPS showed that his office was across the street from a bubble tea shop I had been dying to try, so I was absolutely not checking the internet to figure out how much time I had to get there before it closed.

"Nothing," I chirped.

He looked from me to the computer and back again, the side of his mouth twitching as he asked, "You want me to shut this door and leave you alone for a little while?"

"Why?" I replied flatly. "You know I like an audience when I'm getting myself off."

You didn't live with two men for as long as I had and not learn a thing or two. When it came to jokes about sex, men were still teenage boys. It was all fun and games until a woman—especially one they considered a sister—turned it back around on them.

As I'd hoped, Mark's whole face went up in flames. "Ohhhhhkay, then," he drawled, reaching for the door, his feet already shuffling backward.

Laughing, I stopped him before he could make a getaway. "I'm kidding. What's up? Why were you calling me?"

As always, he recovered quickly. "Brought food home from the bar. You want some?"

Unlike The Wave, The Rusty Nail was a bar through and through. Not exactly known for their food unless it was two a.m. and everyone was plastered, in which case it had three Michelin stars.

I shifted my computer to the nightstand and stood up. "I was actually just about to head out. Can you save me a plate?"

He poked his stomach out, his usually firm abs shaping into a round belly. "I'm going to tell you yes and even go so far as to make you a plate and put it in the fridge, but I make no promises it will still be there when you get home. So, plan accordingly."

Laughing, I walked into my closet. I'd been wearing sandals with my short, cream, lace boho-chic dress while showing houses all day, but the possibility of seeing Bowen again called for an upgrade. "I'll bring home sushi."

"Oh, text me when you get there. I might need some spicy tuna."

I had no idea how Mark stayed in shape. He never stopped eating.

"Will do." I stepped into a pair of wedges and then froze when I saw my cursed maxi dress balled up in the corner, right where I'd banished it as soon as we'd gotten home from the courthouse. Smiling to myself, I remembered the empty spot in Bowen's wallet. Could he really be mad if I stopped by to return the safety pin he'd loaned me and then attempt to hire him for a job that was going to line his pocket? Nobody was upset to see a customer walk through the door. Plus, I owed the man a drink. Maybe Bowen liked bubble tea too?

Coconut milk tea with cranberry pearls was the flavor of the day along with the most decadent chocolate-iced peanut butter cookies roughly the size of my face. I nixed the cranberry for pomegranate—because let's be honest, nobody liked cranberry—and waited while they made half the cookies with no icing just in case someone didn't like chocolate. Assuming Michaels & Company wasn't a one-man show, I went big.

Trust me. Happy employees meant a happy boss, and I had

a sneaking suspicion I was going to need all the help I could get with Bowen.

What? Bribery never hurt anyone.

"Oh, wow," the young blonde receptionist greeted as I walked through the front door, my arms filled with deliciousness. She immediately walked around her desk, saying, "Let me help you with that." Like any normal, logical human, she tried to take the carrier of four teas from my hand first, but they were too precariously balanced for her to be able to grab them without making me drop everything else.

"Wait. Grab this." I turned to the side, performing what I considered to be a damn near heroic juggling act, and angled a box of cookies in her direction.

When I was a kid, my father and I used to play Jenga every Saturday night. He'd drink root beer and put on a baseball game while I set up, and then we'd flip a coin to see who went first. Any abs I had were the product of repeatedly doubling over in laughter as the whole tower fell on my dad's first turn. He. Was. Awful.

And as the woman took the purse dangling from my fingers instead of the box on top, it was safe to say she was equally as horrible at Jenga.

With the unexpected shift in weight, it was a whole hopeless chain reaction. The cup carrier toppled to the left, and in a real Sophie's Choice, I dropped the box of cookies in an effort to save the drinks. Such was my luck, I was fast enough to grab one. Also, such was my luck—it slipped from the carrier, leaving me to watch in horror as the other three exploded against the tile floor.

"Shit!" I exclaimed, milk tea splashing everywhere, red

fruity pearls bouncing around the waiting area like the balloon drop on New Year's Eve.

"Oh. My. God," she breathed as liquid dripped from her pencil skirt.

Right, okay. So, fun fact: Bribery *can* in fact hurt someone.

And then, because it was my life, it got worse.

"What the hell is going on?" a deep baritone asked, the toes of his stylish brown dress shoes appearing just out of the splash zone.

You know, I was really starting to think Karma had it out for me when it came to this man.

Slowly lifting my head, I took my time sweeping my gaze up his body.

Khaki slacks that shouldn't have been that attractive.

Yet another button-down, tucked in at his trim waist and pulled tight over his broad shoulders.

Sexy beard only slightly thicker than scruff covering his chiseled jaw.

Gorgeous full lips that had been the star of a fantasy or two of mine over the weekend.

"Hi," I whispered, a wicked smile curling my mouth.

He stared at me, wide-eyed and slack-jawed, though I couldn't tell if it was because he was surprised to see me or the mess I'd made in his waiting area.

When it became clear he wasn't going to say anything, I did what I do best and filled the silence. "Of all the professions, I never figured you to be an accountant. Though the suit and handkerchief make more sense now."

His Adam's apple bobbed before he let out a low groan. "What are you doing here?"

Extending the one remaining bubble tea, I took a step toward him. "I, um, owed you a drink?"

"Don't move," he ordered roughly.

I froze, my hand still outstretched, which left me looking as much like the fool as I suddenly felt.

"Emily, go get cleaned up and then please see if they have a mop we can borrow next door."

"On it," the receptionist replied, her scowl no doubt leveled on me as she disappeared down the hall, but I only had eyes for Bowen.

Stabbing his hand into the pocket of his slacks, he said…

Nothing. No, seriously, like absolutely nothing. Unnervingly nothing. Deafeningly nothing. *Nothing*.

Once again, that was my cue. "I'm really sorry about this. I have this thing where I don't completely think things through, like say, carrying half a bakery into your office in one trip. At some point, I usually realize it's a bad idea, but I'm already committed so I start to think that maybe I can handle it, but in reality, I can't, so I end up—"

"Why are you here?" he snapped, blatantly interrupting me. In a way, he had also rescued me from the rest of the word vomit I was no doubt going to continue spewing his way, but did he really have to be so rude?

Still, I persevered. "I need an accountant." I took a step toward him. "So I came bearing treats with hopes—"

"Stop. Moving."

I twisted my lips as he interrupted me—again. "Hindsight tells me I should have come without the treats, but I do have money to pay for your services. I'm not asking for a favor or anything. See, my dad, he's retiring to Miami and the accounting for his restaurant is—"

"Jesus," he mumbled, raking a hand through the top of his short, brown hair. "How did you find me?"

Thrice.

Three freaking times he had interrupted me. And considering he had spoken only slightly more sentences, that was an infuriating ratio.

Loaded with saccharine and sarcasm, I smiled. "Do you understand how conversation works?"

"What?"

Using my free hand, I pointed at my mouth. "One person speaks a full and complete thought." I turned my finger on him. "Then, when that person has finished, the other replies. Preferably without acting like a jerk, but we should probably just start with the basics."

Bending over, I picked the box of cookies off the floor. It had broken open when I'd dropped it, but it still had a few that could be salvaged inside.

"Let's give it a shot, yeah? Hi, Bowen. Sorry about the mess in your office. It was an honest accident. I stopped by to see if you were taking new clients because I seem to have found myself in quite the pickle, and I'm really hoping to keep my father out of an orange jumpsuit. Can I interest you in a bubble tea and peanut butter cookie while we discuss the—"

He didn't have to interrupt me that time. I did it all by myself. In my attempt to put him in his place, I slid like an Olympic ice skater.

"Shit!" I shouted, adding another twelve ounces of tea, and what was left of my dignity to the sugary wreckage at my feet.

In one swift movement, he hooked his arm around my hips and plucked me off my feet. His fingertips branded my hip as he turned us and walked only a few steps, but as I dangled at his side, a fire ignited across my skin.

"Dammit, I said not to move," he grumbled, placing me back on my feet.

The loss of his warmth as he released me was staggering, but much to my surprise, he didn't back away. Tall and strong, he crowded me without touching, engulfing me without the first flame. There were plenty of sparks though. Flying in every which direction, singeing my skin. My pulse quickened as he swayed toward me, stopping just shy of his chest brushing mine. The almost tangible intensity in his eyes couldn't have been mistaken for anything other than desire, and damn if that wasn't confusing when combined with his next words.

"Jesus, Remi. You gotta stop."

"Stop what?" I breathed, fighting the overwhelming urge to trace my hand up his chest and curl it around the side of his neck. I could have kissed him. He would have let me. The thunderous storm inside his eyes was all but begging for it as he stared down at me.

I'd only interacted with him three times, for a grand total of maybe fifteen minutes, but I knew, to the core of my soul, Bowen was far too complex for me to make the first move.

So we stood there. My heart pounding the pleas my voice refused to verbalize.

Him staring.

Me contently existing in his hypnotizing presence.

Despite my current Google-and-stalk routine, I wasn't completely insane. It had just been a long time since a man had captured my attention. I'd been single for years, focusing on my career and traveling with Mark and Aaron every chance we got. Aaron always told me I was jaded when it came to love because of what my mom had done to my dad. I wasn't sure if I believed him or not, but it would explain a lot about my virtually nonexistent love life.

So why was my body thrumming with need now? Of all people, why Bowen Michaels? It wasn't his dazzling personality—that was for sure. Barring a handkerchief kink I wasn't aware of, it didn't make sense.

But maybe it didn't need to.

He clearly wasn't all that fond of me, yet he was one breath away from tearing my clothes off too.

I could live with that.

A slow grin tipped one side of my mouth as I repeated, "Stop what, Bowen?"

His heated gaze dipped to my mouth, and so there was no mistaking we were on the same page, I licked my lips.

His eyes flared, and just like that, I had him, hook, line, and—

"All right, we're in business," his receptionist said as the front door swung open. "They had a mop *and* bucket."

We both startled, but I didn't have a chance to blink before I lost him.

Fuck.

My.

Life.

My shoulders fell as he walked over to her, holding the door as she pushed in a yellow rolling mop bucket. Once she was inside, he continued to hold it open.

"Leave that there. I'll clean it up when I get back." He looked at me, cold and distant, my heart sinking immediately. "Come on, Remi. I'll walk you out."

"Can I at least help clean up first? I did kinda make the mess."

"I'll handle it," he replied, sweeping out a hand to motion outside.

Well, okay, then. I guessed I really was leaving.

After tiptoeing around fifty dollars of bubble tea and broken cookies, I grabbed my purse off the desk and dug one of my business cards out. "Sorry about your skirt. Send me the bill for your dry cleaning. It's cute. I'd hate for it to get ruined."

With a warm smile, she took the card. "Thanks. You don't have to do that. It goes right in the washer."

"Oh. Well, then use my number to text me where you got it." With that, I headed to the door, Bowen following me out.

Side by side, we walked together to my car. I really hoped he'd lead the conversation for once, but by the time we reached the hood of my Honda Pilot, the silence was killing me.

"What are you doing tonight?" I peered up at him, using a hand to shield the sun. "Any chance you'll let me make this up to you? Dinner on me?"

He stabbed a hand into the top of his neatly combed hair and let out a sigh. "Look, I can't do this. Okay? I can't be your accountant, I can't have drinks or dinner with you, and…whatever the hell almost happened back there, I can't do it, either. I'm sorry. Questionable plant spending aside, you seem great. Beautiful, smart, funny—the whole package. But this is a me thing." Pressing his palms together like a prayer, he tapped his index fingers to his lips. "I am begging you to please just respect that."

Well, shit. That made me feel like a jerk. I was a forward person, not one to back down in the face of rejection—sales had taught me that. But enough was enough. I didn't have many female friends, but I was reasonably sure Mark and Aaron had never begged a woman to leave them alone.

This wasn't just strike three. That was strike three in the bottom of the ninth. Game over.

It stung like hell, but I couldn't be mad at him. He'd laid it out—blunt and to the point. If anything, it made me respect him even more. Disappointing as it was.

"Okay."

He narrowed his eyes. "Okay?"

"Yeah. Totally. I didn't mean to come across as a crazy woman. I'm not going to lie: You've definitely piqued my curiosity, Bowen Michaels. But if you're not interested, you should never have to beg somebody to respect that."

A sad smile broke across his face. "I didn't say I wasn't interested, Remi. I just said I can't."

I swayed my head from side to side. "See, I'm going to pretend you didn't say that. I don't think my neck can take any more whiplash from you."

He chuckled, and for the first time, I saw a glimmer of a sense of humor. It was like when the sun pops out during a rain shower. But the cold, hard truth was I was still getting drenched in the downpour of rejection.

"Fair enough," he said.

"Right, well… I think that's my cue to go. Have an absolutely beautiful life, and let me know if you ever decide you *can*."

"Absolutely," he muttered, dropping his gaze to his shoes.

I had no idea what was going on in Bowen's life. God knew I had enough shit in my own to know better than to ask questions. The hardest part was we were both walking away disappointed that day.

No one could say I didn't try though.

"Oh, wait," I said, digging into my purse. "I almost forgot. Here." I extended the safety pin in his direction. "Who knows. Maybe there's another girl out there with a cursed dress who will need it one day. Not all heroes wear capes, right? Some just save the day with safety pins."

I expected the confusion that crinkled his forehead. It was a used safety pin for Pete's sake, but I was not prepared for the pure and utter awe that stared back at me.

"What did you say?" he gasped.

I blanched, thrown off by the back-and-forth flow of normal dialogue I was suddenly—and finally—having with him. "Which part?"

"All of it." He didn't wait for me to answer. "You kept that?"

I shrugged. "Kinda. It took me this long to finally get the courage up to touch that dress again. Anyway, I thought you might want it back."

He didn't so much as take it from me as I awkwardly shoved it in his hand.

I had to get out of there. Fascinating as it was, I didn't need to know Bowen's obsession with safety pins. He'd made himself clear, and I had a feeling the more I got to know him, the harder it would be to leave him alone.

"Take care, Bowen."

His face got soft as an honest-to-God smile beamed back to me. "Thanks, Remi."

It was probably for the best that we never went on a date. My bedroom wasn't big enough for all my plants *and* every single safety pin in the world that I would inevitably beg, barter, and steal for him based on that one smile alone.

Though the ache in my chest as I got in my car and drove away didn't feel like the best at all.

chapter TEN

Bowen

Seven months before the plane crash...

"Nooo, you got dressed," I groaned when she slid back into bed beside me, her soft breasts molding to my side.

"Oh, hush." She kissed the underside of my jaw. "We both know you are in no condition for round three."

I rolled into her, tasting her mouth before mumbling against it, "Well, not *yet*. But the night is young."

"Maybe. But you are not." She giggled.

I was only a few years older than she was. The delineation being the jump from twenties to thirties that she never let me forget. I could have been a hundred and that one giggle would have been enough to raise my cock from the dead.

Grinning, I tickled her. "You sure about that, smartass?"

She laughed, loud and breathtaking. "Bowen, stop."

I did. Immediately. Not because my chest wasn't full for the first time in months from seeing her lost in laughter, but rather because I wanted to keep her that way. Smiling. Happy. At peace.

Relaxing onto my back, I pulled her close, sliding an arm under her head. "Okay. But don't say I didn't warn you, Sally. You're going to be in serious trouble in an hour or two."

With a sigh, she draped a leg over my hips and used her fingertips to trace circles on my chest. "Hey, Bowen?"

"Right here, babe."

"You know I love you, right?"

"Of course." Dipping low, I kissed the top of her head. "And I love you too. More than anything."

"Yeah. I know. And, well, I just…wanted you to know… it's okay if you want to love somebody else."

My whole body jerked. From the timid tone of her voice, it didn't sound like she'd intended it as a blow, but it had landed like a TKO all the same.

"What's that supposed to mean?" I rumbled, giving her a pointed squeeze. "I don't want anybody else."

The room was dark, but as she tilted her head back, the familiar tears sparkling in her eyes were unmistakable. "But you might. One day."

"No. I won't."

"You could."

"No. I couldn't."

"You don't know that!" she yelled, abruptly sitting up.

My mouth slammed shut as I studied her face. I was used to the mood swings. The highs and the lows, the jarring confusion when the two suddenly collided. But I was still naked and sated after having spent the last two hours worshipping her body for the first time in months. I was not prepared for an argument. Honestly, I would have done anything, short of agreeing to love somebody else, to avoid it.

"Relax," I said, low and even. "It's okay. We're okay."

"We're not though." She crisscrossed her legs, the inches of space it put between us felt like miles. "You have to be prepared, Bowen. You're a nurturer. It's who you are and who you'll always be. But I may not always be here for you to take care of. You've already quit your job and put your whole life on hold for me." She screwed her eyes shut. "I know you love me, but you're too amazing of a man to simply exist at my side. We stand on very opposite ends of the whole soul mate debate, but what if you're wrong? What if I'm not who you're supposed to end up with? What if there's someone out there who can love you better than I can? I can't stand the idea of you being so caught up in my clusterfuck that you wouldn't even notice them walk by."

Looking back, I should have seen it. I should have read between the lines and heard her cry for help. I should have fucking dragged her to the hospital the very same night. But that night had reminded me what good felt like, what *we* felt like, and I was still basking in the high of having made love to a woman who had my full—and forever—undivided attention. I'd naïvely thought we were at a turning point, not a dead end.

Unwilling to match her intensity, I stared at her for several seconds, waiting for her eyes to open. I didn't want her to only hear what I had to say. I needed her to see me make the promise and then hopefully absorb it so we never had to have this unnecessary conversation again.

Sliding up the bed, I put my back to the headboard and

curled my hands around the sides of her neck. "Babe, look at me."

She shook her head. Eyes still closed. Cheeks still damp.

"Sally," I pressed. "*Look* at me."

In the very next beat, her eyes flashed open, so much fear and pain blazing within. I never got used to it. Seeing her suffer almost broke me. And knowing this time that it was because she was worried about me… Well, that sliced me to the core. I couldn't fix much for her, but this one I could handle.

"I love you. Every woman in the damn world could walk past me and I wouldn't see any of them. But let's just say you decide this isn't working out for *you*. Maybe if me stealing all your covers and forgetting to set the coffee maker the night before becomes too much. All you have to do is say the word and I'll reluctantly get back to looking, okay?"

Her shoulders sagged as she blinked back another round of tears. "I just need you to be happy."

I swiped my thumb over her bottom lip before leaning in to press a deep and lingering kiss to her mouth. "I am happy. Things are hard right now, but they'll get better. We *always* get better."

"Yeah." She exhaled, her relief palpable. "We always do." Leaning back, she retrieved something off her nightstand. "I want you to keep this."

A smile pulled at my lips as I took the silver safety pin from her fingers. "Is this…the same one?"

She nodded. "You've fixed me so many times, Bowen. I want you to have it. That way, maybe one day, I can be the one to fix you." Wrapping her hand over mine, she closed my hand around the silly memento. "Who knows. Maybe somebody else will need a hero one day."

Present Day...

I heard Remi's car door shut.

I heard her start the ignition.

And I heard her drive away.

I saw none of it though because, dumbstruck, I stood on the sidewalk, my gaze glued to the safety pin in my hand.

The safety pin I'd given her.

The safety pin she'd kept.

And the very same safety pin she'd returned. Oh, because why not? As if having a beautiful woman, who I found absolutely mesmerizing—albeit clumsy as hell—and was proving to be as relentless as I was weak wasn't hard enough. Now I had to deal with deciphering between signs from the universe and chance?

What the fuck did it even mean? Who returned a safety pin of all things?

I knew of only one person, inconvenient as it might have been.

After the plane crash, I'd done a lot of cursing the universe. *Why me? Why us? Why her?* It had made no sense, after everything we'd been through—everything we'd *survived*—that I would ultimately lose her.

Sally hadn't believed in soul mates or fate or even a higher power running the show, and she'd found it hysterical that I—Mr. Analytical as she'd called me—did. There was no other way to explain how every step—and misstep—I'd taken in my life had led me to her.

However, if I was subscribing to the theory that fate was dealing the cards, it also meant I had to at least consider how Remi had suddenly stumbled into my life—three times now.

If I'd arrived at the courthouse one minute later, she wouldn't have elbowed me in the face.

If I'd gone straight home after work, she wouldn't have seen me at McMurphy's.

If she hadn't spilled those damn drinks, I wouldn't have had to touch her, reminding me just how fucking incredible it felt to have a woman in my arms.

All of that couldn't have happened by pure chance alone.

It was probably nothing but a crush for Remi. Hell, I wasn't a swamp ogre. It wasn't impossible that a woman found me attractive. That alone would have been easy enough to write off. But there was no denying the Goddamn safety pin. Or the indisputable truth that I *craved* Remi Grey in ways I'd never be able to ignore.

If the universe was once again playing its hand at matchmaking, I couldn't very well sit this one out.

Turning the pin in my fingers, I shook my head. Honestly, why was I even surprised?

"Well played, Sally. Well played."

chapter ELEVEN

Remi

"**J**UST PULL ME OUT, DAMMIT," I SNAPPED AT AARON. Searching for just the right angle, he stood over me, his phone held high, recording as he laughed. "First, I have to document this glorious and completely humiliating moment for you. You'll thank me when you go viral."

I impatiently waved a hand in his direction. "I swear, if you post this on TikTok, I'm firing you as my best friend."

He slanted his head and shot me a grin. "Are you really in a position to be making idle threats right now?"

Being that I was stuck half in, half out of the crawl space under a house, it was safe to say I was not in the position for anything other than being cocooned for eternity in a spider's web.

I huffed. "I should have called Mark."

Aaron folded over, put his hands on his knees, and peered into the small space around me. "Could there be snakes in there?"

"I'm not sure, but there will be snakes in your bed tonight if you don't help me up. Come on. I'm losing circulation to my feet." It wasn't true. My feet were fine, but it was safe to say my gray silk blouse would never be the same.

This was what I got for doubting the home inspector when he'd put in his report that the floor to the downstairs bathroom was rotting out. He was in fact correct, by the way. Though I'd missed the part in his write-up about how the hell he'd gotten out of the crawl space. For all I knew, he had pulled the same Winnie the Pooh maneuver on the other side.

"Hurry up. My clients will be home any minute."

"Okay, okay," he said, tucking his phone into his back pocket and then grabbing my hands.

It took a few attempts, him pulling, me wiggling, but eventually, he dragged me free. Mulch was permanently embedded in my shirt, but my pants would dry clean okay.

"Thank you," I said, brushing myself off as best as I could.

He grinned. "No, no. Thank *you*."

"Don't you dare tag me in that video."

He slapped his chest with feigned innocence. "Who, me? Why, I would *never*."

I collected my clipboard off the porch and gave him a side-eye. He would. He had. And with my luck, he'd do it again before we even pulled out of the driveway.

My phone rang as we walked to our cars, Grey Realty flashing on my screen. I glanced at Aaron one last time. "Think before you post, Lanier. Don't forget: I have a video of you ironing pantsless, singing Brooks and Dunn's 'My Maria' like you were auditioning for *American Idol*."

His mouth fell open and his eyes squinted in challenge.

I waved him off as I put the phone to my ear. "Hello."

"Where are you?" Amber, Grey Realty's head administrative assistant/intern/college student/social media specialist, whispered across the line.

"I'm leaving the Maplewood house. What's up?"

"Well, um, it's almost six and I need to clock out, but there's a man in the waiting room. What am I supposed to do?"

My forehead crinkled as I climbed into my car. "What man? And why are you whispering?"

She kept her voice low. "I think his name is Michael Bowen or something. I can't remember. He told me not to bother you, but he's been waiting for over an hour for you to get back here and I have an appointment at the tanning bed at six-thirty. What do I do?"

"I don't know a Michael Bo—" The words died on my tongue as a huge smile stretched my lips. "*Bowen Michaels?*"

"Maybe? Hot guy, dark hair, beard, seriously wicked eyes."

"Suit?" My stomach somersaulted.

"White button-down with the sleeves rolled up. He brought a cactus."

At that, something fluttered a little farther south. Not at the cactus part, though it was curious. There was literally only one look sexier than a suit, and every woman knew exactly what it was.

Apparently, Bowen Michaels knew too.

"I'm on my way. I'll be there in ten."

The drive to my office was short. I spent the whole time trying to make myself somewhat presentable. It was a lost cause. I looked like hell, but my house was in the opposite direction, so a trip home to shower, shave, pluck, ladyscape, brush my teeth, do my hair, apply fresh makeup, and lastly change clothes was out of the question.

But realistically, the last time he'd seen me, I was covered in bubble tea. Mulch was par for the course at this point.

I'd been a realtor for years, but I'd only recently opened my own office. From a financial standpoint, we didn't *need* a storefront, but I had big plans to expand and take on other agents, so I'd rented an end unit at a strip mall with room to grow. Mark and Aaron had helped me move in, but everything in the office had been either painted, planted, or handpicked by me. I was proud of the little space, but never had it stolen my breath before until I walked inside and found Bowen sitting in a cream club chair surrounded by the rainforest phase B.

"Bowen?" I said with enough surprise in my voice to keep Amber out of trouble. I'd been on the receiving end of one of his glares. There was no need to throw her under the bus for having called me. "What are you doing here?"

He stood, his tall, muscular frame unfolding. I waited for the frown. It seemed to be his specialty when it came to me, but as his gaze held mine, his expression remained soft. Not quite a smile, but definitely progress.

"Hi," he said, staring for a beat before grabbing a small potted cactus no bigger than my cell phone off the table and extending it in my direction. "I brought you this." He glanced around at the plants hanging in the corners, his gaze lingering the longest on the massive string of pearls plant, its vines several feet long. "Seems lackluster now."

I bit my lip. "No, it's gorgeous." Our fingertips brushed as I took it from him and I willed the heat rising inside me not to hit my cheeks. "Thank you. This is unexpected after yesterday." I turned the pot from side to side. "Wait. Did you tuck a restraining order in here somewhere?"

He chuckled and my head snapped up, ready and eager for the heart-stopping show that was a Bowen Michaels smile. His whole face beamed. His brown eyes were warmer than before, and his enchanting grin revealed what was possibly a dimple hiding in his neatly trimmed beard.

It did not disappoint.

Amber suddenly appeared at my side. "All right, Remi, I'm out of here. I'll see you in the morning."

I didn't tear my gaze off Bowen as I replied, "Have a good night."

"You too," she sang, the front door swinging shut behind her.

A pregnant silence blanketed the room as we stood there. I'd led every single conversation Bowen and I had ever exchanged, but letting him take the lead would be fun for once. Especially since he'd basically told me to kick rocks the day before.

His Adam's apple bobbed as he wedged his hand inside the pocket of his navy slacks, which were tapered at the ankle and capped by stylish brown dress shoes. "I was hoping we could talk."

"Sure. What's up?" I hooked my thumb over my shoulder. "Do we need privacy? Nobody's here, but I can lock up and we could go to my office."

He shook his head. "That's not necessary. This won't take but a minute."

I couldn't help it. The damn cactus had gotten my hopes

up. Hopes of what, I wasn't quite sure, but his impending brevity made my shoulders sag. "Oh, okay."

His jaw muscles ticked as he drew in a deep breath, and just as he had done too many times before, his gaze cut over my shoulder. "Look, I owe you an apology. The courthouse, the bar, yesterday—that's not me. It's just…" His eyes returned to mine. "I lost my fiancée in the plane crash. And honestly, Remi, most days it feels like I'm drowning."

I nearly dropped the cactus when I slapped a hand over my mouth. Memories of me all but throwing myself at this grieving man raced to the front of my mind. "Oh, God, I'm so sorry. I had no idea. I never would've—"

"Remi, no." Surprise, surprise, he'd interrupted me, but this time, I didn't mind.

Seriously, how could I? I'd been practically harassing a widower.

His long legs devoured the space between us. "I didn't tell you so you'd feel guilty. You didn't do anything wrong. Let me explain myself." His right hand landed on my hip, giving me a warm squeeze.

At the contact, we both froze, and I held my breath, waiting for him to realize he was touching me and then snatch it away like I was again made of fire.

My pulse quickened as his left hand came toward my face ever so slowly. My lungs burned, pleading for oxygen, but there was none to be found in the small space between us.

"Bowen," I managed to whisper.

Dear God, he was going to kiss me.

He'd told me his fiancée was dead, and now he was going to kiss me. The whiplash with this man was not for the faint of heart. Worse, I didn't know what it said about me, but I was going to let him. Right there in my office. Still holding a cactus, I was going to let him do whatever the hell he—

He picked a stick from my hair.

The teasing smile tipped one side of his mouth. "I think you're sprouting branches."

"It's mulch," I replied breathily, even to my own ears.

He squinted one eye. "You take this plant thing pretty serious, huh?"

Okay, yes. That was a much better answer than admitting I'd gotten stuck under a house. "Very, very seriously."

He smiled, bright and white. It was even more attractive up close. "I'll keep that in mind."

"For what?"

"What do you mean for what?"

"I mean, yesterday, you told me you *can't*. I respected it then. But I get it more than ever now. I never should have put you in that position."

"Nope. Don't do that." He gave my hip another firm squeeze. "You don't get to hijack my apology. Just listen."

He was too close for me to listen. Too close not to read into every single move he made. And even knowing that he was about to let me down easy all over again, he was too damn close for me to not want more.

I needed space from this man so I could feel like a decent, empathetic human being again. "Any chance I can put Quincy down first?"

His lips twitched. "Quincy the cactus?"

I shrugged. "It feels right."

His eyes darkened, his smile slipping away as he leaned in close. "It does, doesn't it?"

Chills exploded across my skin and my mouth dried. It was not fair that he had that kind of effect on me when I was so obviously trying to be respectful of his situation. Okay, maybe not *that* respectful. I arched my back, causing my breasts to brush his chest.

What? Hell was probably more fun anyway.

He let out a low growl before thankfully—and unfortunately—backing away. "Right. Okay. Talk first."

First?

I was more intrigued by what came second.

I set Quincy on Amber's desk. I'd move him to my office later. Cacti weren't really my thing, but this one might give Margret a run for her money as my new favorite. "I'm listening."

He cleared his throat. "I think I may have misspoken yesterday when I told you that I *can't* do this with you. I thought about it—*you*—a lot last night and I've come to the conclusion that the better statement is I don't know *how* to do this." He rubbed the back of his neck. "You have to understand, my life has been a maze of tragedy for the last year or so. If I'm being honest, I lost my fiancée long before the plane crash, but in a lot of ways, I'm standing in that maze, still searching for a way out. Yesterday, as you drove away, I realized that locking the door didn't keep you out as much as it just kept me inside that much longer."

My chest ached for him, and I fought the urge to reach out and touch him in a way that couldn't possibly ease his pain. My hands never moved, but he must have sensed my intentions

the difference between SOMEBODY and SOMEONE

because he offered me a sad smile and lifted one long finger in the air, asking for me to wait.

"You don't know me," he said, "but I'm asking for a chance to change that. Just dinner. Drinks. Let me run you off the good old-fashioned way with riveting conversation of tax law and military history. If it doesn't work, it doesn't work. But I have too many regrets in my life to allow a missed opportunity with you to become another." He smiled shyly, so completely unlike any version of Bowen I'd seen before. "So, I guess, long story short: Would you like to…go on a date with me?"

I stared at him, wondering what kind of horrors lurked in the shadows of his maze. It wasn't my place to ask him. Not now. Not yet.

Crossing my arms over my chest, I slanted my head. "So, that's it? That's your sales pitch? Tragedy, mazes, and military history?"

"I'm afraid so." He smirked, rocking from heel to toe. "Oh, and I can do whatever kind of accounting it was you needed help with."

He hadn't had to offer me anything. I would have said yes regardless. But he didn't need to know that. "Free of charge?"

"Mmmm." He swayed his head from side to side. "I heard something about your dad and an orange jumpsuit. The consultation is free, but I make no promises about the rest."

My hand shot out so fast that I heard it whiz through the air. "Deal."

Bowen's grin as we shook on our arrangement was almost as wide as my own.

chapter
TWELVE

Bowen

OVER THE NEXT TWO DAYS, TIME MOVED IMPOSSIBLY SLOW. Remi and I had exchanged numbers and agreed to meet at a little sushi place near her office after her open house on Saturday afternoon. A day date wasn't exactly ideal, but it was necessary for where I wanted to take her.

It was now Thursday, and I still hadn't heard from her. For as much as Remi talked, I assumed some of that would translate into at least one text over the course of the week. Though it wasn't like I'd texted her, either.

I'd picked up my phone several times. I'd even opened up a message addressed to her. I'd typed little, but I'd sent even less. I was so out of the game when it came to dating that I didn't know where to start. *Hi* was the classic carefree-yet-obvious-I'm-interested-a-healthy-amount option. Though I feared my fingertips would follow it up with *I can't stop thinking about you,* which would no doubt erase any cool-guy foothold I had. It was safer if I said nothing at all.

So that was what I did. Torturous as it might have been.

As I finished up for the day, I dreaded going home. It shouldn't have worked like that. Home should have been my escape. But my nephews had soccer on Thursdays not far from my house, so Cassidy always stopped by to make sure I was still breathing. Today was no exception. She'd already sent me pictures of Sugar and Clyde sunbathing in their favorite spot in the backyard. They loved her, but personally, I could pass on the weekly interrogations, especially now that I had something—*someone*—to hide.

There was a knock on my office door and then Emily cracked it open. "Hey, Remi Grey just dropped off some paperwork for you. She said it was her father's receipts, but it looks like a bag of trash and smells like French fries."

It was comical how fast I lurched to my feet. "She's here?"

"Well, she was. Don't worry. No mop needed this time."

I hurried past her to the waiting area. "Why didn't you tell me?"

"Um...because you have specifically told me not to bother you when a client stops by unannounced."

I let out a low growl and marched to the front door, hoping I could catch her. And say what? I had no idea, but I'd figure it out. I trusted my mouth slightly more than my fingertips.

I scanned the parking lot for any sign of her. The disappointment that she'd been so close was a sucker punch to the gut—until I caught sight of a white Honda Pilot parked in front of the tea shop across the street. There was no mistaking the succulent hanging in a crocheted net on the rearview mirror.

Earlier that week, I'd cursed that shop for over an hour as I'd crawled around on my hands and knees, chasing fruity pearls from under the chairs. As I stepped off the curb, a smile on my face, I was all too happy to eat my words.

She was standing at the counter when I quietly walked inside. Her long, blond hair cascaded down her back, and tight jeans hugged the curve of her ass.

"That will be nine sixty-two," the barista told her.

In one fluid movement, I retrieved my wallet, slid my credit card out, and extended it over Remi's shoulder. "I've got it."

She spun around, a beautiful mixture of surprise and delight on her pretty face. "Hey," she said.

The barista took my card.

Remi tried to stop her. "No, wait. Don't run that. I owe *you* the drink, remember?"

Ignoring her, I jerked my chin for the barista to continue. "Actually, you bought me four drinks, and I think we can all agree it was more than enough."

A soft laugh escaped through her perfect lips. "Fine. What about a cookie, then?"

"Thanks, but I'm good. I can't eat anything from here. Peanuts."

Her eyes flashed wide. "Oh my God, you're allergic to nuts? I could have killed you with those cookies on Monday." She patted my chest down like she was searching for an injury. "You didn't eat any, right?"

I grinned—only partially because her hands were all over me. "Off the floor? Tempting as it might have been, no. But yes, I am allergic. They just give me hives, not send me into anaphylactic shock."

She peered up at me, more serious than I'd ever seen her. "Do you carry an EpiPen just in case?"

"I have one in my office, yes."

"Then you have to teach me how to use it before our date. I can't carry your demise on my conscience."

I chuckled. There was a high probability this woman was going to be the death of me, though I didn't think it would involve a single peanut. "Fair enough. You free now?"

"Sure. Give me a second." She turned back to the counter. "Ma'am. Sorry. I'm actually not going to need that cookie after all."

I rested my hand on the small of her back and dipped low, putting my lips to her ear. She smelled intoxicating, like wildflowers and honey. "It's not a big deal. You should have the cookie."

Her breath hitched and she arched into my touch. "That's okay. I'd rather keep my options open without the added risk of killing you."

I didn't quite understand until she tipped her head back, her cheeks pink, her gaze heated and aimed at my mouth.

Yep. Fuck the cookie. For that matter, fuck the EpiPen, the ten miles between us and my house, and Atlanta's indecent exposure laws too.

"Good idea," I murmured.

The barista cleared her throat and handed me my card back, shaking us from the moment. Then she kindly switched out Remi's dessert for a second tea. It was a beyond horrible mix of cherry and milk, but as we walked back to my office together, I sipped it with pride.

Remi watched me with rapt attention as I taught her to

use the EpiPen, which I belatedly realized was long expired. I'd never actually had to use the life-saving device, but the fact that she cared enough to learn was cute. She'd gone so far as to open her phone a few times to take notes.

In the face of crisis, I would be grateful for the ease and speed in which an EpiPen could be administered. Though, in the face of desperate need to spend more time with a woman, the ten minutes it took me to teach her how to use it was woefully short. Then again, any amount of time with Remi eagerly on her knees, rubbing her hand against my thigh in broad daylight, would never be enough.

The things this woman did to me were dangerous in all the right ways.

"And that's all there is to it?" she asked before hopping up to sit on the corner of my desk, facing me.

I fought the urge to walk over and stand between her legs. My hands would have wandered. Then my mouth. Instead, I sank into my rolling chair and inwardly praised the surprising amount of control I'd managed to muster through the hands-on emergency tutorial. "Just make sure you've called nine-one-one and that's it. You feel better about our date now?"

She slanted her head and shot me a warm smile. "I don't know. I guess that depends on where you're taking me."

"Well, I figured we'd start the day with something exciting like taking my truck in for an oil change. After that, we'll rob a liquor store, hijack a train, and knock off a few banks. Really, the possibilities are endless."

Her eyes lit. "You drive a truck?" A smile slid around her face as she sucked her lips into her mouth, failing to hide it.

I barked a laugh. "That's what you took from all that?"

She popped one shoulder. "I just didn't picture you as a truck guy."

"But you can picture me as a fifties mobster?"

She crossed her arms over her rounded chest. "Bowen—hot as you may be—you're an accountant with a peanut allergy, who carries a handkerchief. It was safe to assume the rest was a joke."

"Hey!" I laughed and matched her body language, folding my forearms over each other, loving the way she watched. I flexed my bicep for good measure, causing her to swallow and then regain her composure in the blink of an eye. "Are you calling me a nerd, Ms. Grey?"

"I don't know yet, Bo," she retaliated only to cringe. Clearly not liking the sound of the condensed version of my name, she corrected with, "Bo*wen*, tell me more about this truck?"

I leaned back in my chair and crossed my legs, again pleased with how I could distract her just by moving. "It's silver. Four wheels. Power locks and windows. And if I'm not mistaken, it has an engine *and* a transmission."

She hummed. "Wow, both? I had no idea you were such a gearhead."

I laughed again, shaking my head. "And I had no idea you were such a smartass."

"I guess we're learning a lot today, aren't we? Me with my medical qualifications, and you with…" She inched over on the desk so her dangling feet hit my outstretched legs. "Your newfound knowledge of thirst trapping. You know what you're doing, Sir Flex-A-Lot."

Busted.

"Is it working?" I winked and waited for her to either throw me a bone or lie through her teeth.

"Let's just say, minus your whole hives thing, if you don't take it down a notch, I might be the one who needs a crash cart." She bit her lip and looked down at her lap. "Which is why I should probably get going."

Funny, only days ago, I couldn't make Remi leave me alone, and now I would have made deals with the devil himself for another hour.

"Or you could stay."

Her head popped up, the same excitement swirling in my chest reflecting back at me in her blue eyes.

"I promised you a free consult. I haven't had a chance to look through your dad's stuff yet, but I don't have anywhere to be tonight if you don't."

She looked at her watch and I wondered if maybe I'd gotten ahead of myself. After all, if she'd wanted to hang out and go over things, she wouldn't have just dropped off the paperwork and darted away.

However, I'd already walked out to the ledge, and there I waited.

Throwing me a line, she answered, "Only if there's pizza. I've already sacrificed a cookie for you. A girl's gotta eat."

It was dinner time in a busy area of Atlanta. Getting a pizza delivered was going to take forever, but I did not give a single shit if it meant she'd stay.

"Done." I stood up and gave her leg a squeeze before I started toward the bag Emily had set on my filing cabinet earlier.

It took two hours for our pizza to arrive, and in that time, we barely even made a dent in her father's records. How the man was still in business was a mystery that may never be solved. By the time we stopped to eat, we weren't to the point where an actual CPA was even useful yet. It had been all organizing, deciphering, and scanning. And if she had been any other client, Emily would have been delegated this part of the process.

But it was Remi and she had yet to stop talking, chattering away and charming me all the while. Which basically meant I had yet to stop smiling. I was going to be sore as shit the next day. My strained facial muscles did not know how to handle the rare workout.

"So, you live with two guys?" I asked, dragging my second piece of pizza onto a paper towel.

She sat on top of the table in my conference room, her legs crisscrossed with piles of papers stacked around her. "Yep. Contrary to popular belief, men and women can be friends. I've known them since high school, and nobody's ever fallen in love or into bed with each other. So it's not nearly as scandalous as you'd probably assume."

I smirked. "I'm not assuming anything."

"Most people do." She pinched a section of cheese off the top of her pizza and popped it into her mouth, chewing and swallowing before inquiring, "Tell me something about Bowen Michaels. You've got to be sick of listening to me prattle on about myself by now."

I wasn't. Not even close.

I propped my feet onto the chair beside me. "What do you want to know?"

"Everything."

"That's a tall order."

"Yes, okay. Let's start with that. How tall are you really?"

"Six-four."

She nodded multiple times. "Okay, very nice. And do the other nerds know you work out?"

I wanted to laugh, but I wanted to hear hers more than my own. "I mentioned it in the group chat once. They have assured me my pocket protector is not in jeopardy."

Just as I'd hoped, her laughter was musical. A whimsical symphony that would no doubt be on a loop in my head for the foreseeable future.

God, it felt *good*.

Being there with her. Happy and free. I hadn't felt either of those emotions in what felt like an eternity.

Remi was fascinating. I was cataloging her details one hundred percent more than her father's financials.

Her favorite color was purple.

She loved to travel almost as much as she loved spending a Friday night on the couch, rewatching old seasons of *The Bachelor*.

She liked white wine, not red.

And any given Sunday, she could be found pretending to do yoga in the park. As she was actually there to people watch.

"Favorite restaurant?" she asked.

"Mai Thai." I pointedly raked my gaze around the room. "Though I hear you can eat free at The Wave."

She laughed. "You better start working on your sob story now, Michaels. Unless you have—" Horror hit her eyes for a blink before she buried her gaze in her lap. "Never mind."

And there it was. I didn't need to ask for clarification. It had been two days since I'd told her about Sally. A part of me wondered how she hadn't asked me more about her already.

"It's okay," I said, sitting up in my chair and discarding my half-eaten slice on the table. "I'm well aware I have a four-course-meal-worthy sob story. Don't be embarrassed."

"I didn't mean to bring her up." She popped her head up, looking thoroughly flustered as she stumbled over her words. "I mean, bring *it* up. Like the plane crash. I don't like to talk about it, either." She let out a groan. "That's not true. I've actually found it really therapeutic to talk to Aaron about it. And if you ever want to talk about it, I'm happy to listen. I just don't want to force you or anything if you aren't comfortable." She paused and stared at me. "I'm going to stop talking now." Then she pulled an imaginary zipper across her pouty lips.

Chuckling, I stood up and moved around the table. I caught her legs, turned her, and slid her to the edge. I did not delay in stepping into the open space between her thighs. "Relax." With my thumb and my index finger, I unzipped her imaginary safeguard. The light pass over her mouth caused her lids to flutter. "You didn't say anything wrong. One day, we'll have to talk about the plane crash. It's a part of both of us. But it doesn't need to be tonight."

She nodded. "Since I've kinda already opened the door, can I ask you something before we shut it again?"

My palms slid over the curve of her hips, drawing her even closer. "Of course."

"How do you know you're ready to move on? From her."

My hands stilled and the muscles in my back strained. Son of a bitch. After such a good night, this was about to fucking suck. "I don't."

It was her turn to stiffen, but her fingers wandered up my forearms to my biceps. "Thank you for being honest."

My gut wrenched. "What I do know is that today, tonight, has been incredible. *You* have been incredible, and I've loved every minute of being here with you. You deserve a better answer than what I just gave you. But if you're willing to give me a little time, I'm going to work so damn hard to get my head straight and figure it out."

"Okay," she whispered, looping her arms around my neck. "That's fair."

I shook my head adamantly. "No. It is absolutely not fair to you, but it's all I have right now, Remi."

She smiled, gliding her fingertips up the back of my neck into my hair. "Then that's enough."

I wanted to kiss her. I wanted to lay her out on the table and lose myself, make the world cease to exist outside that conference room. I wanted to give her everything I had, but not like this. She deserved the entire fucking world, not half a man who was drowning in the past.

"We should finish organizing this stuff before it gets too late."

"Yeah. That is definitely the best use of our time right now," she replied breathlessly.

It probably made me an ass, but her disappointment was seriously sexy.

chapter
THIRTEEN

Remi

It was past nine when Bowen walked me to the door. His conference room was a wreck of my father's papers, and I felt guilty for abandoning the mess, but he'd called it controlled chaos and told me to leave it until he had the chance to log everything the next day. It was a much bigger project than I had ever imagined. Certainly bigger than a free consult. The smirk he was wearing when I asked him to send me a bill for his time told me not to hold my breath. But I was persistent. The fact that the man who had rejected me thrice now had his pinky hooked with mine as he held the door open for me was proof.

"Thank you," I said when we got outside. I needed to go home. I had a meeting with a new client at eight the next morning, a date night outfit to shop for as soon as the mall opened, and then a full afternoon of showing houses to an out-of-town couple.

I didn't want to leave though.

My body had definitely been on to something when it reacted to Bowen at the courthouse. Above and beyond the fact that I could have stared at the sexy man all damn night, he was seriously amazing in every other way as well. Kind and funny. Witty and smart.

Trust me. It was hard to find a man who could keep up with my sarcasm. But he did, and it was an even bigger turn-on than the whole rolling-up-the-sleeves thing. And I'd be remiss if I didn't note that the flexing had been driving me crazy all damn night. I wanted in those arms.

Luckily, his handkerchief hadn't made another appearance, so I'd been able to keep myself in check—for the most part.

"No, thank *you*," he replied as the door swung shut. "I'm glad I was able to convince you to hang out with me tonight."

I looked down at our tangled fingers. "I don't know how much convincing it took, but I'm glad you did too." The parking lot was empty except for my SUV and a new, silver extended-cab Chevy in the corner. A grin broke across my face. "So the truck is real."

He chuckled, and it didn't matter how many times I'd heard it that night—it pleasantly surprised me each time. "Yep. Don't forget to wear comfortable shoes for our bank heist on Saturday."

Laughing, I swayed into him.

He dropped my finger and wrapped his arm around my shoulders. As I'd imagined, it felt safe and good. He had me in height by at least a foot, but with me pressed against his front, we were the perfect fit. I took a minute to absorb his warmth before forcing myself away. As much as I hated to go, leaving was the only way to speed up to the weekend.

He walked me to my car and waited for me to unlock the

door before pulling it open like a gentleman. From Bowen, I wouldn't have expected any less.

"Be careful driving home."

"I will," I chirped.

I tossed my purse onto the passenger seat and started to climb in, when a thought pulled me up short. I hadn't said it earlier during our brief discussion about the plane crash, but it felt wrong to leave it unspoken.

"Hey, Bowen?"

"Yeah," he replied, grinning down at me.

"I want you to know that you can take all the time you need…ya know, getting your head straight. I can tell how much you loved her, and that's never a bad thing. If you ever feel up to talking, I'd love to hear about her someday."

His smile fell immediately, but I didn't regret saying it. It was important to me that he knew my concern about him moving on wasn't out of jealousy. I didn't know him well yet, but I wanted to. And if that happened, a day would come when he'd have questions about my past too. I couldn't expect acceptance and understanding without first offering the same to him.

"Anyway…I just needed you to know that. Have a good night, Bowen."

When I started to get into my car again, his hand came down on my arm. The tug he gave me, turning me to face him, wasn't rough, but it definitely wasn't gentle.

And neither was his mouth as it came down over mine.

A low growl vibrated in his chest, and my body hummed as he palmed the side of my face, his tongue exploring my mouth with a tangible desperation. I moaned, clinging to his sides as he guided me backward. I had no idea how he could still be spatially aware as he ravaged my mouth with the most erotic kiss of my entire life, but he turned our bodies so my back gently landed against the rear door.

His chest came flush with mine, his entire presence engulfing me in heat, branding me in ways I'd never be able to explain.

I couldn't breathe.

I couldn't see.

All I could do was feel him consuming me with every stroke of his tongue.

Little by little, the frenzy slowed, but even when he did finally break the kiss, he didn't move away. "Remi," he panted into my mouth.

"That's me," I panted back for lack of better words. Or, ya know, thoughts in general.

His quiet laugh breezed across my skin, and then he was back to kissing me—deep and dizzying.

I didn't know how long we stood there, mouths fused, hearts pounding. It could have been hours just as easily as seconds. Regardless, it wasn't long enough. As fast as it had started, with one final peck, it was over. He took my hand and pulled me away from the car, his other arm folding around my hips. But it wasn't the same without his mouth.

"Remi, look at me."

Boneless, I sagged in his strong arms, my lids fluttering open.

Bowen stared into me, a storm brewing in his eyes. It wasn't quite angry, but it was unsettling all the same.

"Are you...okay?" I asked.

He searched my face, a slow and tangible inspection. "Are you?"

"Mmmm, your pocket protector might be in danger of being revoked after a kiss like that, but yeah, I'm pretty damn sure I'm just fine. I think this is what the accounting world calls a swoon surplus."

His Adam's apple bobbed, and then whatever kiss-induced trance he was in vanished. One side of his mouth hiked a fraction. "You're lucky I have a new affinity for that sexy mouth, smartass." He pinched my side. "Now, go. Get out of here, and text me when you get home so I don't have to worry."

I smiled. "You don't have to worry about me."

His eyes got dark, but he took my hand, brought it to his lips, and kissed the back. "Really? Because I'm starting to think you're the only thing I should be worried about."

I bit my bottom lip.

I could have stood there with him all night. It didn't matter that we were in a parking lot. Or that I would have gotten no sleep. I would have been with Bowen, and that would have been more than enough. But at his urging, I slid into my car. I grinned huge when he leaned in one last time, pecked me on the lips, and closed my door. Then he stood on the curb, watching as I drove out of sight.

Damn. Why was Saturday so far away?

~

As soon as I climbed out of the car, I pulled my phone from my purse. There were several messages from clients that I'd missed while hanging out with Bowen and at least six from Aaron all with various degrees of "Where the hell are you?" But seeing as Aaron's Lexus was parked next to my SUV in the driveway, I decided to text Bowen first.

Me: I'm home.

His reply was almost instantaneous.

Bowen: Good. Now try to get some sleep.

Me: You too. Thanks again.

Bowen: No need to keep thanking me. The pleasure was all mine.

I wasn't sure I agreed with that. The way he'd pressed me against the car, his mouth moving over mine, his hands teasing my sides... Well, it was all pretty damn pleasurable for me. I didn't feel the need to tell him any of that though. I was still grinning like a maniac when I walked into the house.

Aaron, on the other hand, was *not*.

"Where the hell have you been?" he snapped, suddenly sitting up on the couch, his plaid pajama pants sticking out from under a throw blanket.

I curled my lip. "Oh, hi, Aaron. So good to see you too."

"Don't give me that crap. I was worried."

I smiled. It seemed to be a running theme for the evening. Though, as twisted as it might have been, I liked the idea of Bowen worrying about me. With Aaron, it was just annoying.

I lifted my hands and turned in a circle. "As you can see, I'm fine. I had some... *work* I needed to finish up."

"I called your office."

Uninterested in playing a game of *whose day was it to watch me*, I gave up. "Okay, fine. You caught me. I was out with a wildly attractive man who kissed me breathless and awoke a sexual desire within me that I never knew existed."

He rolled his eyes. "So you're just not going to tell me at all?"

I laughed at the irony and kicked my shoes off as I walked over to the couch. Flopping down beside him, I gave the blanket a hard tug. "So, what are we watching?"

He glared at me for a few more seconds but eventually scooted over, fluffing the blanket so it covered both of us. "I was trying to call you because the settlement amounts came out tonight."

I swung my head in his direction. "What? Tonight? I thought they wouldn't be ready for at least another week?"

He shrugged. "I think they want this over. I ended up with six hundred thousand dollars."

My jaw unhinged. "Holy shit."

"Yeah. My thoughts exactly. You should check your email."

It had never been about the money for us. Aaron and I had agreed from the start that a good portion we were awarded from the settlement would go right back to a fund for the families of those who had lost their lives. There were too many children who had lost parents, husbands and wives widowed, and families torn apart to ever benefit from the profit of their losses.

As a group of twenty-seven survivors, we'd decided the money should be divided on a sliding scale and allowed our attorneys to hire an outside company to objectively make those decisions. Those who were injured the worst and would likely require long-term if not permanent care would receive the most compensation. Aaron had been one of the few to walk away with minor injuries, so six hundred thousand dollars was far more than he'd been expecting. However, I had convinced him to submit the records from his therapists. Not all injuries were diagnosed in the emergency room. Survivor's guilt was a very real condition for him.

I hooked my arm with my best friend's and leaned my head on his shoulder. His anxiety when I'd gotten home suddenly made a lot more sense. A pang of guilt hit me when I realized he'd been alone when he read that email all because I'd been too preoccupied with Bowen to answer his texts.

Shit. Bowen.

Based on the time stamp on my email, they'd been sent while the two of us had been flirting and eating pizza. He hadn't so much as touched his phone when we'd been together. That meant he too was going to be opening the email alone—if he hadn't already.

It wasn't the day to talk about the plane crash. I'd already crossed the line by mentioning his fiancée before I'd left. It had led to a smoldering kiss, but I didn't think checking up on him and opening that door after he'd so clearly told me he wasn't ready was going to garner me the same results this time. But I couldn't very well ignore the fact that he too was a survivor.

I offered Aaron a tight smile. "You want a glass of wine?"

He lifted one shoulder. "I already took my meds, so I'll have to settle for another cucumber water." He swiveled, retrieved a glass from the end table, and then passed it my way.

"You made cucumber water?"

"Don't give me shit. It was healthier than the handle of tequila I reached for first."

"Excellent point. It is late. Maybe I'll have some cucumber water too." Carrying my phone and his glass, I walked to the kitchen and backed into the only corner not visible from the den. Then I typed out a message.

Me: Hey, I should probably confess now that I'm really bad with locked doors. I just realized the settlement emails were sent today. If you ever feel the need to knock, I'm here.

Bowen: I don't give a shit about doors, locked or not. If you need something, I'll rip it off the damn hinges. Are you okay?

I smiled down at my phone. That was a little…aggressive but also super sweet.

Me: I'm fine. Aaron's struggling a little tonight. I wanted to make sure you were good before I disappeared to hang out with him.

Bowen: Don't worry about me. I spent my evening with a beautiful woman who is utterly intoxicating. It's going to take far more than a settlement email to get me down. Take care of your friend, and call me if you need anything.

My chest warmed. It was good to see Bowen put the same energy into being charming as he had into being cranky.

Still grinning, I refilled Aaron's glass and made one for myself before once again joining him on the couch.

"I hope you made it stiff," he said dryly, taking the drink from my hand.

"Double cucumber. I even picked out a slice of lemon just for you."

"Oh, goodie." His voice was full of contempt. "Open yours and let's see how many orphaned kids you'll be able to put through college."

I hated every part of this, but the sooner it was over, the better.

For all of us.

I opened the email and clicked on the link. It took a few minutes for me to verify my identity, but as soon as I hit enter, both of our jaws dropped.

Two-point-nine million dollars.

"Oh my God," I breathed.

He let out a groan. "It's still not enough."

He was right, but the damage had been done. This money would make a difference in the lives of a lot of people. Including my own.

Unfortunately, the future was the only thing I could change.

chapter
FOURTEEN

Bowen

Eight months before the plane crash…

THE SHRIEK OF MY PHONE RINGING ON FULL VOLUME STARTLED ME awake. A week of exhaustion clung to my mind, and it took several beats before razor-sharp reality rained down over me, slicing me to the core. I had no concept of what time it was. After yet another long night of fruitlessly searching the city, I'd only lain down for a minute. But the sun, which had been tucked behind the horizon, now poured in through my bedroom windows.

"Hello," I rasped, scrubbing a hand over my face.

"They found her," Tyson said, his voice barely above a whisper.

That was all I'd needed to kick-start my heart again. A tsunami of adrenaline flooded my system. "Is she okay?"

"She's…alive."

Sally. Oh, God, Sally.

An avalanche of relief crashed down over me.

It had been five days since she'd disappeared.

Five agonizing days of losing my mind and assuming the worst.

Five whole damn days since I'd been able to breathe without it feeling like my lungs were full of broken glass.

"You gotta give me more than that, Ty." I stabbed my feet into a pair of running shoes and headed toward the front door.

"She was brought in by ambulance. Her vitals are good, but they found her in her car, down by the trails on Grove Hill. The EMT gave her Narcan, but—"

I froze mid-step. "Wait. What the fuck are you talking about?"

He blew out a hard breath. "Did you know she was an addict?"

I shook my head, nothing making sense. "That's impossible."

"I would have said that too, but you haven't seen her. She's covered in track marks. If she wasn't using regularly before she disappeared, that's all she's done since."

"There's no fucking way. I would have known. I would've noticed something."

"Would you? You've been together for, what, a month now?"

"I would have fucking known!" I boomed, my voice echoing around my living room as I marched into it.

No, we hadn't been together long. It was the same bullshit her friends and family had given me over the last few days while I'd flipped the city on end trying to find her. But I fucking knew her in ways no one else ever would. We were two halves of the same whole, and I didn't need to spend a Goddamn decade with her to know it. She was my forever; the rest would come later.

"There must be another explanation," I told my brother. "I've searched Grove Hill every day this week. If she was there this morning, then where the hell has she been for the last five days?" I slapped a hand down on the counter as I rounded it on the way to the door, grabbing my keys. "What hospital are you at?"

"Do *not* come up here. Do you understand me? I could lose my license for calling you. Besides, the cops won't let you see her. They still have to question her, and I'll be honest, it wouldn't surprise me if they placed her under arrest, either."

"Arrest? She's been missing for almost a week. Those sons of bitches wouldn't even help us look for her, but now they're going to *arrest* her? For what?"

"She was found with heroin, Bowen. *Heroin*. Depending on the officer, he might brush it under the rug, but he could just as easily take her in. I'm sure the cops will notify her family. Wait to hear from them before you come up here. I'm not even supposed to be in the ER today. A buddy did me a solid when he heard they brought her here. I'd really rather not thank him by getting him fired."

I gritted my teeth, not slowing as I stomped outside. "Look, I don't know your friend, and this call never happened. But you have to tell me where she is. I've spent too long in absolute hell, terrified something happened to her. I don't give a fuck what the cops say. They can arrest me too for all I care. But I have to see her, Tyson. So either you tell me what hospital or I drive to every fucking emergency room in the city until I find her."

"Jesus," he hissed. "Can you give me, like, five minutes to think before you dive off the deep end here?"

"Tyson," I warned as I reached my truck.

"Chill. She's safe, okay? You barging in here like a madman won't help anyone. Not even her."

He was wrong. Seeing her was the only thing that could help me. I'd been drowning in what-ifs. Mainly because we couldn't actually convince anyone she was missing in the first place.

It had taken two days of begging to even get the police to acknowledge her disappearance. When they'd shown up to search her place, there was no sign of anything amiss. Her suitcase was nowhere to be found, but it explained why a few of her drawers had been emptied. Her car was gone. Purse and cell phone too. But in my gut, I knew that something wasn't right. She wouldn't have left without telling me. Without saying goodbye.

However, once it was discovered that she'd left a message at her office explaining how she was taking the rest of the week off, law enforcement had written us off altogether. According to them, a woman who had obviously decided to go on vacation hardly constituted a missing person.

I'd never stopped looking though.

I'd just never expected to find her like that. *Fucking hell. Heroin?*

It didn't matter. My love for her was not conditional. I wasn't a praying man, but I'd done my fair share of it on my knees that week, and her being okay was the answer to every single one of them.

"I'm not asking again, Tyson. What. Hospital?"

He let out a low groan. "Grady. But just…give me a minute."

"I don't have a minute!" I yelled, but it did me no good. He'd already hung up.

I tore out of my driveway like a man on the verge of destruction, and in a lot of ways, it was exactly who I was.

Tyson spent the majority of his time at Grady, but it wasn't unheard of for him to be at one of the other area hospitals. Grady was the biggest though, so I figured it was safest to start there.

Much like my life, traffic was a nightmare. Even without the slow-down, it was going to take me well over half an hour to get there, but I didn't get more than a few miles from my house before my phone started ringing again, my brother's name showing on the screen.

Lifting it to my ear, I answered with, "I swear to God, if you don't give me—"

"Bowen?" she cried, her voice weak but still the most beautiful sound I'd ever heard.

"Sally," I breathed, barely able to speak around the emotion lodged in my throat. "Are you okay?"

"I don't know what's happening," she rushed out. "You have to believe me. I didn't do this. He…he drugged me."

My head snapped back as I steered to the shoulder of the road, hell-bent on getting to her but not trusting myself behind the wheel anymore. "Who?"

"I don't know." A sob tore from her throat.

"Shhhh. It's okay. Just breathe." I wasn't following my own advice. My lungs burned like a wildfire was raging inside them as I asked, "Are you saying someone *took* you?"

"Yes! The last thing I remember is going for a run at Grove Hill, and after that, it's all blurry. He kept me in a dark room, and it was so damn cold. There was another girl too, and she cried the whole time. I think she might have been hurt, but…I don't know." She took a shuddering breath. "It's all flashes. I have no idea how to sort them out."

I'd known it. I'd fucking known she hadn't taken off for a few days the way the police had insisted. But this was one thing I'd never wanted to be right about.

My chest filled with flames and every fevered muscle in my body screamed with visceral rage. I cracked my neck and flexed my hand open and shut on the steering wheel, desperately trying to keep my tone gentle. "Did you tell the police? They should be out searching for this motherfucker."

"I've tried, but they won't listen to me. They keep asking for details and I don't have any. I don't know who he was or what he looked like. I don't know where he took me or how he got me there. I just know it happened. I'm pretty sure they think I'm making it up too, but I swear on my life I'm telling the truth!" She was on the edge of hysterics, and with her next words, she took me right over the cliff with her. "What if they won't listen? What if he comes back for me? I don't even know why he let me go."

"No!" I said entirely too sharply. I bit the inside of my mouth so hard that it drew blood and then lowered my voice. "That's not going to happen, babe. You're safe now. Everything's going to be okay." It was a bald-faced lie. Nothing would ever be the same again. But I would never, *never* stop trying to make it the truth. "I'm on my way. We'll figure everything out, I swear."

"I love you," she choked out.

"I know, Sally. I love you too."

chapter
FIFTEEN

Remi

"Technically, yes, it's a three-bedroom. But the bonus room can easily be converted into a fourth if you need more space."

The young couple looked at each other, so much love in their eyes that cartoon hearts might as well have been floating over their heads.

"I think this is the one," the woman told her husband.

"Yeah?"

She nodded eagerly, her brown hair brushing her shoulders.

Looking back at me, he said, "Okay, then. We'll have our agent draw up an offer."

"Great. I look forward to it." I smiled.

He smiled too. His wife giggled and buried her face in his chest.

They were cute. I really hoped their offer came in higher than the other four sitting in my email, but I said none of that.

With his arm around her shoulders, he was already on his phone as they trotted down the front steps.

Ah, young love.

Sighing, I turned around and scanned the empty space. It had been a busy open house, but things had finally slowed down. I had another two hours before I was supposed to meet Bowen for our date, but I needed to tidy up, put away the snacks I'd brought, and then head back to my office so I could go through the offers first.

"Knock, knock," a familiar baritone said.

I spun to the door, a smile already spreading across my face. "Hey..." More words were supposed to follow that one, but that was before Bowen Michaels walked in wearing a fitted black V-neck T-shirt that hugged his defined chest and a pair of jeans that hung low on his tapered hips.

He was gorgeous in a suit.

He was sexy in a button-down and slacks.

He was downright edible in a white button-down with the sleeves rolled up.

But casual, easy-breezy Bowen no doubt left a trail of gaping, flush-faced women in his wake. I was nothing but his latest victim.

Though I might have had it worse than most since he was holding a stunning Swiss cheese plant that had to be at least half as tall as he was.

Like icing on the sex cake, the side of his mouth hiked. "You busy?"

Instinctively, I smoothed the top of my hair. "Not anymore. What are you doing here?"

He looked at the green tree, which was in a rich-amber pot

propped on his hip. "I wanted to bring you flowers for our date, but I'm still recovering from the embarrassment of giving you the world's smallest cactus."

Touching my fingers to my lips, I stifled a laugh. "Don't hate on Quincy."

"No hate, but I definitely learned that bigger is better when it comes to buying you foliage."

"Just so you know, 'bigger is better' applies to practically everything when it comes to women."

He shook his head, his smile stretching wide. "I also learned that Sharon at Peachtree Plants might be a hundred and six, but she has no shame in pinching a man's rear end if she finds it aesthetically pleasing and the mood strikes her. I was in no way prepared for plant people, Remi."

All the hands in the world wouldn't have been enough to stifle my laughter that time. "Well, she isn't wrong. You do have a particularly *aesthetically pleasing* backside. I may have checked it out a time or two myself."

Bowen quirked his eyebrow and with slow, calculated steps closed the distance between us. "It can't be that good. After all, you've managed to keep your hands to yourself." He stopped so close I had to crane my head back to hold his gaze.

"What I lack in verbal restraint, I really make up for in grab-ass."

He let out a low hum. "That's unfortunate to hear." And with that, he moved the massive plant from between us, dipped low, and placed a chaste but no less toe-curling kiss to my lips.

"You're supposed to kiss me at the end of the date," I challenged, hoping and affirming I'd get another.

"Well, I also brought you a three-foot tree instead of a bouquet. It's safe to say I'm breaking all the rules tonight."

I couldn't wait for later, so I pushed up onto my toes and stole another kiss. "You warned me you were a rebel."

His smile against my mouth was almost as good as the kiss itself, but somehow, I managed to break the connection.

Dropping back to my heels, I ran my fingers over the Swiss cheese's leaves. "She's beautiful, Bowen."

"It looked half-dead like Margret, so I figured it must be nice."

"Well, aren't you a quick study. She's a Monstera too. She and Margret are practically sisters."

"I hope it's okay I stopped by. Amber gave me the address. I didn't want you to have to lug…" He paused, slanting his head in question, waiting for me to fill in the blank with the name of the newest member of my plant family.

"Meredith."

"Right. I didn't want you to have to lug Meredith around with us all night. I figured you could drop it—I mean, *her*—off at your office."

I smiled. "You know you could have dropped her off at my office instead of driving all the way out here."

"But then I wouldn't have been able to see you or find out about your pervy obsession with my ass."

I winked. "It sounds like we both won here."

"Yeah," he whispered, staring deep into my eyes. It was a far cry from the man who only a week earlier refused to make eye contact. But then again, nothing about Bowen was the same as when I'd met him.

I'd been attracted to him when I'd thought he was broody

the difference between SOMEBODY and SOMEONE

and stoic. But this guy, the one who made jokes and brought me plants... Well, he was better. So, so, so much better.

A voice came from the front door. "Is the open house still going?"

I peeked around Bowen and found an agent I'd worked with in the past standing beside another starry-eyed couple. "Yeah, absolutely," I chirped. "Come on in."

Bowen dipped his head. "I'll let you get back to work."

I took Meredith from his arms and gave her a spin to really check her out. "You did good, Bowen. Way better than flowers."

He grinned. "Good. Now don't ogle me in front of your potential buyers when I walk away."

I shrugged. "Sorry. I make no promises."

Chuckling, he gave my hip a squeeze. "See you at three?"

"I'll be there."

"I'm counting on it." Turning on a toe, he walked away, nodding at the agent and the couple as he went.

And despite my attempts to always remain professional in front of clients, I made no secret of watching his ass the entire way.

I hurried through the last showing. They weren't nearly as interested when they found out it only had two bathrooms, but it worked out just fine when I saw the offer in my email for five thousand dollars over asking from the young couple from earlier. The sellers were equally as stoked and accepted immediately.

When Meredith and I got back to Grey Realty, I found her a temporary spot in my office. Quincy Cactus had pride of place on my desk, but regardless of what Mark and Aaron had to say about it, Meredith was coming home with me.

After I'd uploaded the offer into the digital signature

software and emailed it to my sellers, I closed my laptop and mentally shifted gears. I was going straight from my office to the date with Bowen, so I'd planned ahead, wearing a cute jade strapless dress with a cropped brown blazer for a daytime look. But I shed the jacket to showcase extra skin for the afternoon and evening. I didn't have much time to freshen up, but I spent the little I did touching up my makeup and straightening my hair. Bowen had already seen me, but conversely, I'd also seen him, and there was no way I was resigning myself to be the troll at the dinner table.

Miraculously, I wasn't even late as I walked into the restaurant. Well, assuming the fifteen-minute grace period at my doctor's office applied to dates as well. The restaurant was predictably empty for three p.m., but there was only one man who truly mattered and he was leaning against the wall near the hostess stand. When his gaze locked on mine, the hairs on the back of my neck stood on end.

I had no idea what he'd been doing since I'd last seen him a few hours earlier, but he'd changed clothes at some point. His jeans were darker and tapered at the ankle, and his untucked button-down was almost nautical with a fine blue-and-white stripe. But once again, Bowen had employed the male species secret weapon and rolled his sleeves up his forearms.

A slow, sexy grin curled his lips as he shoved off the wall and strolled my way. "There she is." He leaned in for a half hug and pressed a gentle kiss to my cheek.

I far preferred the familiarity of the one he'd placed on my mouth back at my open house, but I would never complain about Bowen's lips touching any part of my body. He was so close that a new cologne he hadn't worn before filled my senses.

"Mmm," I moaned. "You smell amazing."

"Yeah?" he asked, eyeing me closely.

"Wait. Is that…" I drew in a deep inhale, scanning my mind to identify the fragrance.

He stared down at me expectantly, his eyes twinkling with something I couldn't quite pinpoint.

"Oh, oh, wait. Is it Hugo Boss?"

His eyebrows shot up. "Versace, but not a bad guess."

"Damn. I'm usually good with colognes. I buy some for the guys every year at Christmas. Aaron tries to overcompensate with brute and woodsy scents when everyone knows he needs the more clean, understated-masculinity fragrances. Mark, on the other hand, has been wearing the same sports spray since high school. Even then, it was awful. I'll never have nieces and nephews if I don't get those two married off soon."

Resting his hand on the small of my back, he guided me to the hostess stand. "I have two nephews you can borrow. The seven-year-old is a ventriloquist who never leaves home without his dummy, and his nine-year-old brother insists on breaking at least one limb every summer. So that's fun."

He didn't say anything to the hostess. Instinctively, she grabbed two menus and guided us to a small table in the back. Once we were seated and drink orders had been taken—New Zealand Sav Blanc for me, whiskey neat for him—we jumped right back into conversation, never missing a step.

"A ventriloquist? How cool is that?"

Bowen smiled, his chest puffing with pride. "It's actually really fun to watch. He's super talented too. My sister is hell-bent on making the boys play every sport under the sun, but I've never seen Preston happier than when he got a vintage Charlie Chaplin dummy for his birthday."

"Stop it. There's no way a seven-year-old knows Charlie Chaplin?"

He nodded enthusiastically. "Did I mention he also listens to smooth jazz and drinks apple juice from a chipped teacup? He's a character. That's for sure."

Warmth filled my chest. It was nice to see another side of Bowen. I didn't have a big family, but while we had been working on my dad's taxes, I'd filled his ears with stories of growing up at The Wave and meeting Aaron and Mark. He'd listened but hadn't offered up much about his own life that night. So, as our drinks were delivered, I hurried to keep him talking.

"Okay, so we have Preston, and what is nine-year-old Harry Houdini's name?"

"Simon." He rolled his eyes. "Simon Reginald Harrington the Third."

"Oh, wow. That's..." *Pretentious.* I clinked my glass of wine with his whiskey and tipped it back to avoid finishing the thought.

He laughed. "Funny enough, my mother had a similar reaction when she heard it for the first time too."

I got comfy in my seat and fiddled with the stem on my glass, prying for every last detail he'd give me. "And your parents. Are they still together?"

"Disgustingly so," he replied, shaking his gorgeous head.

"And just one sister? Older? Younger?"

"Older. I have a younger brother too."

I nodded and kept going, filing everything away under *Basics of Bowen 101.* "Originally from Atlanta?"

"Born and raised."

"College?"

"Georgia."

"Yes!" I lifted my hand and high-fived him across the linen-covered table. "Go Dawgs."

Rich laughter escaped his throat as he caught my hand. Intertwining our fingers, he rested them on the table. "I told you this wasn't speed dating, right?"

Appreciating how our fingers looked linked together, I conceded. "Yeah. I know. I just like learning about you. Usually, I'm the talker."

"I've noticed, but guess what?"

"What?"

"I enjoy listening to you talk." He looked down at our hands and smiled almost…shyly? Yet another facet of the mystery that was Bowen Michaels.

I stroked his thumb with my own, thinking about how much things had changed—improved tenfold—between us. "You're different."

His head popped up, a mixture of surprise and curiosity crinkling his forehead. "How so?"

"I don't know. When I met you, you were so distant and hollow. I wasn't completely sure you possessed the facial muscles to smile. But now"—I pointed to his mouth—"it seems like you've mastered the task pretty well."

"It's not that I didn't know how to smile. It's just that it's been a long time since I had a reason to."

Heat flooded my cheeks and I attempted to hide it by taking another sip of my wine. "That was smooth, Mr. Michaels."

He chuckled. "The fellow nerds will be thrilled to hear it."

I narrowed my eyes. "Were you talking about me in the group text again?"

"Maybe."

"Good. Keep it up."

I loved the back-and-forth with him. The fact that he could laugh at himself was a huge turn-on. Even more so than V-neck-casual Bowen. What I loved most was, despite the way things had started, there was an effortless comfort between us that I'd never felt with a man—at least not romantically speaking, and sure as hell not on a first official date.

Just when I thought he couldn't get any better, the waitress arrived to take our dinner order, but I hadn't even picked up the menu. Luckily, I didn't have to.

Bowen ordered a boat.

No, seriously. A literal boat of sushi intended for four people, complete with steamed dumplings, edamame, tempura veggies, and enough sushi to feed a small army—or fleet, rather. It was a first date and I was now practically required to stuff my face because everyone knew leftover sushi didn't keep.

He looked over at me. "Anything you'd like to add?"

It was a little too soon to ask for his hand in marriage, so instead, I looked at the waitress. "Is the tempura cooked in vegetable oil or peanut oil?"

"Uhhhh..." she drawled.

Robust laughter bubbled from Bowen's throat. "Remi, relax. I've eaten here before."

"Oh, okay." Releasing his hand, I passed my unread menu to the waitress. "Can't be too safe."

"You are so right," he replied, thoroughly amused.

I liked how he was as entertained by me as I was by him.

the difference between **SOMEBODY** and **SOMEONE**

Swirling my wine glass, I asked, "Where are you taking me this fine afternoon?"

"After the reaction I got from gifting you Meredith earlier, I'll be staying on theme with a trip to the botanical gardens."

"Shut up. Seriously?"

He nodded. "You've probably been a million times."

"Actually, I've *never* been. I've always wanted to though. Thirty acres of outdoor gardens, Bowen. It'll make Peachtree Plants look like an herb garden. Your aesthetically pleasing rear could be in real danger."

He shrugged. "As long as you're willing to watch my six, I should be fine."

"Oh, I'll definitely watch your six, seven, eight, and nine. For a trip to the botanical gardens, I might even pull a Sharon and pinch your six too."

"Money well spent." He winked. "Wait a minute. Let me get this straight. You own a plant that cost more than your rent, but you've never made it across town to the holy land?"

"The whole horticulture obsession is kinda new. I didn't get into plants until—" *Shit.* I shifted awkwardly in my chair. "So a boat of sushi, huh? How hungry are you?"

"Since the plane crash?" he said, filling in the blinking, neon blank.

I lifted my hand in surrender. "Door shut. Still locked." I tossed a ball of air over my shoulder. "Threw away the key."

His lips thinned. "It happened, Remi. Just because I'm not ready to talk about it doesn't mean you have to avoid it completely. It's bound to come up from time to time."

Swallowing hard, I offered him a tight smile. "I know. With

everything you've been through… I didn't want to make you uncomfortable or anything."

He leaned forward and once again caught my hand. "The only thing that's going to make me uncomfortable is you tiptoeing around me, giving me the highlights of you, when I want the whole damn experience. So let's try this again. You got into plants after the plane crash, right?" He circled his free hand in the air, signaling for me to continue.

I crinkled my nose. I could lie and take the easy way out, sparing us both, but I didn't want to do that with him. The plane crash had changed my entire life. It was a massive part of who I was. He probably wasn't ready for the full experience the way he claimed, but I could gently wean him in.

"I was in the hospital for a while. Tons of people—some I didn't even know—flooded my room with flowers. As sweet as it was, I hated them. I was stuck in that hospital bed, day after day, forced to watch them wither away. After all the lives that were lost, I couldn't stand dealing with more death." I paused to get a read on him. One of those souls had worn his ring and owned his heart. I didn't know her name or what she'd looked like, but if this man loved her, she must have been incredible.

Confident from the earnest way he was listening, totally focused, I continued. "It was the opposite with the potted plants though. A little water every day and they thrived. In the most sterile setting imaginable, I watched them grow and flourish. Everything that I'd felt was impossible back then. When I was finally discharged from the hospital, Mark and Aaron had to make three different trips down to the car to carry all of them. They begged me to donate some, but by then, they were my babies." I gave his hand a squeeze. "You did good with Meredith today. In my opinion, clipped flowers are overrated. There's nothing worse than watching something so beautiful wither into nothingness."

Maybe I'd gotten ahead of myself, because his face grew dark. The storm brewing within him when we'd met returned to his eyes. Even from the outside, the destruction being caused by that hurricane was catastrophic. But still, he stared at me. His gaze searched my face as if I held the answers to every question he'd never spoken. It made me a terrible person, but my stomach dipped at the thought that I had even one answer for him.

Never breaking his intense attention from me, he brought our joined hands to his lips and peppered kisses over the back. "You have no idea how right you are about that."

On his next exhale, the clouds in his eyes faded. "Right, so… A boat of sushi. Hope you brought your appetite."

I grinned across the table at him, thankful the bleak moment had passed. "Dibs on the sashimi."

Like the morning sun coming over the horizon, his face lit again, and just like that, Bowen came back to me.

"You better be quick with the chopsticks then, Ms. Grey."

The rest of dinner was easy and breezy, the way a first date should be. We ate *a lot*. Laughed even more. Teased each other relentlessly. It was by far the best date of my life, and the best part was it wasn't even over yet.

When we finally finished all we could and he paid the check, I rode with Bowen to Atlanta's Botanical Garden, where we spent the rest of the afternoon strolling hand in hand through a horticultural heaven. He knew almost nothing about plants, and I was almost positive he didn't care, either. But I never would have known based on the smile on his face as he listened to me prattle on for hours.

I didn't want the night to end. Though the moan-inducing goodbye kiss as he dropped me off at my car softened the blow. He made me promise to text him as soon as I was home, but when I pulled into my driveway, there were already a half dozen notifications on my screen.

Bowen: So, I know tomorrow is Sunday and all, but would you want to come over and watch the baseball game with a nerd??

Bowen: The Braves are away, but I could fire up the grill.

Bowen: Or we could order in again and skip the game completely.

Bowen: Movie maybe? Here or a theater?

Bowen: Yeah, we could definitely go out again if you're more comfortable with that than coming to my place.

Bowen: And please…when you get home and read these, can we not discuss how I just sent you four thousand consecutive texts to ask you out on another date?

I giggled as I started typing.

Me: First of all, I love baseball. But are you grilling burgers or brats?

the difference between **SOMEBODY** and **SOMEONE**

Bowen: After I saw the way you devoured sushi tonight, we're probably gonna need both.

I laughed again, my cheeks strained from a day full of it.

Me: Then yes. I would love to come over and watch the game tomorrow night. Sadly, there is no way I can ignore, nor forget, your text-a-thon. I think you like me, Mr. Michaels.

Bowen: All calculations on my end seem to add up that way. I've been going over the stats since I watched you drive off. Which, for the record, was my least favorite part of the evening.

Me: Well, statistically speaking, I can assure you the rest of the date put all your numbers in the red.

Bowen: What? Red isn't good.

Me: Oh, well, I guess I'll leave the mathing to you. Regardless, please report back to the nerds that our feelings are mutual. Also…I just got home.

Bowen: Excellent news on both fronts.

Me: Thanks again for an amazing day. Sweet dreams.

Bowen: I'm not sure how sweet they'll be, but they will all be of you.

Heat rushed through my body, nipples to clit.
Oh. My. Gawd.
This man. Mr. Tall, Dark, and Nice Ass. The Man of Mystery. He was becoming Mr. Sweep Me Off My Feet.

chapter SIXTEEN

Bowen

"ARE YOU AVOIDING ME?" MY PAIN-IN-THE-ASS SISTER ASKED across the line.

After wedging my phone between my ear and my shoulder, I pulled my sheets out of the dryer, answering, "Let me get this straight. You have been riding my ass for the better part of the last six months to get a life and today I call you to tell you I'm having a friend over for dinner and your conclusion is that I'm avoiding you?"

She scoffed. "Fine. Then tell me about this *alleged friend*. Are they imaginary? Go by the name Clyde or Sugar? Or is this more of a Calvin and Hobbs situation?"

I walked to my bedroom, dropped the sheets onto the chair in the corner, and then got busy with the stretch-and-smooth routine to make up the bed. "First, you're an ass. Second, it's actually a client." No lies detected.

"A client you'd like to keep? Because—no offense—Bowen, I've had your cooking."

I glared at the wall, hoping she'd somehow feel it at her house twenty minutes away. There was only one way to get her off my ass. It would take exactly one pronoun to ensure I had my house all to myself, completely uninterrupted, for a solid twenty-four hours. The problem was, on the twenty-fifth hour, all hell would break loose, and the entire Michaels family would descend upon me like the first wave of the zombie apocalypse, starved for details rather than brains. Though, if I wanted to guarantee I didn't get any surprise visitors while Remi was over, I had to give her something.

"Oh, no offense taken, and thanks for your vote of confidence, but I'm sure *she* will love my burgers."

The line fell silent just as I'd assumed.

"Oh my God," Cassidy breathed. "You're having a *woman* over? For *dinner*?"

I folded the top sheet back and dragged the midnight-blue comforter up the bed. "Yeah. So call off your dogs. I don't need Tyson or Mom or Dad stopping in to check on me tonight—or, hell, at all anymore. In fact, spread the word. Everyone should return their keys and give me some privacy in my own damn house again."

"Wait. Wait. Wait. Is this like…a date-date?"

"I hope so. Otherwise it's going to be real awkward when I try to kiss her."

"Oh my God!" she shouted at a decibel I feared would wake the dogs.

When the pillows were neatly stacked on the bed, I replied,

"Okay. That's enough. God himself has now heard about my date. Give the man a break."

"Spill it. What's her name? What's she do? How did you meet?"

"See, this is exactly what we are *not* going to do right now. I only told you about it because I need all of you to give me some space to explore things with her. *Some well-deserved privacy.* Then—if and when the time comes—I'll tell you guys everything, but please just lay off and let me do this on my own."

She let out a groan of frustration. Relinquishing control was not Cassidy's strong suit. "Fine. Then at least tell me how serious it is."

Really fucking serious.
Life-changing serious.
Terrifyingly serious.

"It's all very new, Cass," I answered. "Give me a little time to figure it out. That's all I'm asking for."

"Fine," she huffed. "But whenever you're ready to talk about her, I want to be the first to know. Tyson does not get the first call. Do you hear me?"

I chuckled. "Loud and clear."

"Good. Now go Google how to make a decent burger so you don't give the poor girl botulism."

Shaking my head, I grinned. "Love you too."

"I *do* love you. And in all seriousness, I'm proud of you. This is exciting. I hope your secret woman realizes how lucky she is."

Yeah. My sister loved me. But she was dead wrong. I was the lucky one. "I appreciate that."

"Have fun tonight."

"Will do."

After a round of byes, I hung up and sank onto the bed. Remi was supposed to arrive in an hour, and while I'd tidied up the back porch earlier in the day, I still had a few things to do around the house to get ready.

Most importantly...

I reached for the picture frame on the nightstand and traced my finger over the face behind the glass. Sally's smile was bright and carefree as she sat on my lap, both of us tipsy on wine and drunk in love. It had been taken not long after we'd met, but in so many ways, it felt like a lifetime ago. We were all smiles and laughter in those days.

After the plane crash, the picture had felt like a rusty blade lancing my soul. The what-could've-beens taunted me every time I caught sight of her face. Half the time, I kept it tucked away in a drawer so I didn't have to look at it. There were days when the memories hurt too much for me to breathe. But then other times, I needed to see it. *Her*. I needed to remember the woman she'd been before she'd disappeared so I could be at peace knowing she was no longer living in a constant state of fear.

She would have hated the way I'd shut down and allowed the darkness to consume me.

She'd wanted me to be happy. She'd said it herself. Sometimes over and over.

And this was my chance—Remi was my chance.

Guilt churned in my stomach as I stared down at the woman who would always own a part of my heart. You didn't travel through hell with someone for them not to become sewn into the fibers of your life.

the difference between SOMEBODY and SOMEONE

But those days were gone—just like Sally.

If I had any hope of moving forward, I had to stop looking at the past. Life didn't move in that direction.

"I'll find you again," I whispered. "Somehow, someway. But until then, this has to be goodbye." The image of her smiling back at me, a moment of immeasurable love and happiness, trapped in time. Where it would forever stay. Swallowing hard, I carried the frame to my closet and retrieved a box of her belongings tucked in the back. I'd thought about putting it away for good at least a hundred times.

But today was different. *I* was different.

For the first time, I had hope again. Maybe fate hadn't wronged me after all.

Without further hesitation, I opened the box and placed the picture inside on top of a stack of sweaters she'd bought for Sugar. It hurt like hell, and the fragile pieces of what was left of us in my heart crumbled, but the relief of letting go as I closed the lid—and ultimately the hardest chapter of my entire life— was overwhelming.

I was free.

We were free.

Almost exactly an hour later, and fifteen minutes late, there was a knock at my front door. Grinning, I smoothed my Braves T-shirt down and took one last glance around the house to make sure everything was in place. Burgers were seasoned to perfection and molded into patties. Lettuce and tomatoes were prepped— no onions though. Brats had been soaked in beer, and the baked potatoes had been wrapped in foil and baked, ready to be crisped on the grill.

The only thing missing was her.

I pulled the door open and found Remi standing on the welcome mat, holding a six pack. She was wearing tight jeans, ripped at the knees, and a cropped, white Braves jersey showing off a mouth-watering strip of skin at her stomach. Her blond hair was braided into pigtails, the top covered by a backward navy-blue baseball cap. She was always sexy, but damn, she could pull off sporty too.

Her smile grew as she took in my shirt. "I briefly panicked on the way over that you were a Red Sox fan and I'd never be able to speak to you again."

"My father would have disowned me if I was."

"I like him already."

She stepped inside, and then I shut the door behind her. Taking the beer from her, I slid my free hand around her waist, splaying my fingers across the warm bare skin on her back.

Her smile faded as my mouth came down to cover hers.

I had intentions of keeping it chaste. However, as her lips parted, her tongue gliding with mine, it seemed Remi had other plans.

I had to admit that her approach was far superior.

"Mmm," she hummed into my mouth, linking her fingers behind my neck and bringing our bodies flush until her breasts pillowed between us. "I love that you don't wait until the end of the night to kiss me."

"Patience is not a virtue I possess when it comes to you."

She nipped at my bottom lip. "Good. Don't start now." She pecked me one last time before releasing me.

I watched as she strolled into the open living room, dining room, and kitchen area.

She trailed her finger over the modern handcrafted mahogany end table. "I should have known better than to picture you having a cheesy bachelor pad, but I'm impressed."

I carried the beer to the kitchen and popped them into the fridge. "My sister's an interior designer and insisted on decorating the place as soon as I bought it a few years back." I pointed to the gray overstuffed sofa and love seat with built-in recliners. "Those are my style." I swept a finger through the room, allowing it to linger on the abstract black-and-white canvases hanging on the walls and the red art deco floor lamp in the corner, which my sister claimed was the pop of color the room had been missing. "And the rest is what she *thinks* my style is."

She meandered over to the bar dividing the rooms and slanted her head. "If you don't like it, why don't you change it?"

"Because she's not wrong. It looks way better than anything I would've put together. You want to see something that is totally my style though?"

"Absolutely." Her eyes danced with a contagious excitement that spread through my chest.

I scooped up the tray of raw burgers, balancing them on one hand, and then walked around the bar. "Come on. I should probably start cooking anyway."

Taking my free hand, she followed as I led her out the back door. While it wasn't quite dark yet, the sun had sunk below the horizon, triggering the warm glow of solar lights draped from one end of the porch to the other.

Cassidy had had a field day decorating my house, but I'd forbidden her from touching the outside. In Atlanta, finding a unicorn was more likely than stumbling across a large, secluded, partially wooded backyard. I'd fallen in love immediately, long before I had ever known I'd one day need a place to escape the devastation inside both the house and myself.

What started as a simple covered porch had turned into a sanctuary. I had an outdoor kitchen, complete with a grill, a small built-in pizza oven, and a natural-stone wraparound bar. There was a seating area just outside of the covering, where I did the bulk of my reading—and grieving. Off to the right was a stone walkway leading to a smokeless firepit, and on the other end, mounted on the wall beside the door, was a fifty-inch TV. But my favorite part, especially after seeing Remi's face light up when she saw it too, was the plush bed swing covered in a mountain of pillows.

"Oh, wow," she breathed. "This is gorgeous."

It was. One hundred percent. But having her there made it exponentially better.

I jutted my chin toward the swing. "Remote's over there. Turn on the TV and find the—"

"Oh, God!" she screamed, scrambling backward in a panic.

Her back slammed into my front, which popped the hat off her head and knocked the plate of burgers from my hand. I was too stunned by her sudden outburst to be able to catch them before they flipped to the ground. The plate let out a teeth-jarring crash as it shattered, but all of my attention was homed in on Remi as she scaled my body, frantic to get away from… what? I had no idea.

Adrenaline surged through me, her flight response skyrocketing my fight. I looked up, ready to take on whatever fucking grizzly bear was so obviously headed our way, only to find Clyde trotting toward us.

Acrid guilt hit my stomach.

"Shit. I forgot. They're not going to hurt you." Hooking her around the waist, I guided her behind me and snapped my fingers at the dogs. "Sit."

Clyde immediately slowed, walking the rest of the way over. He picked up Remi's hat in his mouth before dropping down on his ass in front of me. Sugar wasn't far behind him, and manners were a work in progress for the little guy, so I bent down to scoop him up.

I put my chin to my shoulder and peered back at her. "You okay?"

Her chest heaved and her hand, fisted in the back of my shirt, loosened a fraction. "I, uh, think so?"

"Okay, well, take a deep breath. You are a hundred percent safe. I'll put them both in the house, but I need you to move over to the swing so I can get to the door. Can you do that for me?"

"Y-yeah," she stammered, but even as she started shuffling over, she held my shirt, turning me with her, using me like a shield.

Tugging the hat from his teeth, I caught Clyde by the collar, his tail wagging full throttle, and I waited for Remi to release me before guiding him around the broken plate and spilled meat and into the house. I needed to lock them up in the guest room, but I wanted to check on her first. So, once they were inside, I quickly shut the door, grabbed the entire doormat, folded it in half, and dumped the shards of glass and the majority of our dinner into the trash can by the grill. Then I gave my full attention back to her.

Pale-faced and wide-eyed, she had crawled into the stack of pillows, only her shoulders and head sticking out. I would have laughed if the adrenaline ebbing in my system had left me able to process anything other than her fear.

"Jesus, Remi. I am so sorry." I tossed her slobbery hat onto the bar and then sank down on the edge of the swing and started digging her out. "I wasn't thinking... I—"

"No. It's fine. I should have warned you. There was a huge dog next door when I was growing up. He used to get out all the time and chase me into the house." She tugged the neck of her shirt to the side, revealing a flat white scar several inches long. "He finally caught me once when I was twelve. Scared the absolute shit out of me. There was blood everywhere. I thought I was dying. It didn't end up being too bad, but I've never been comfortable around dogs since. Especially if they sneak up on me."

As if on cue, there was a thud at the back door and she let out a squeak, once again ducking back behind the fluffy cushions.

Clyde had squeezed his large body under the blinds on the door and had his snout pressed against the glass. Sugar joined the circus, tap-dancing on his back legs while attempting to paw his way out. Honestly, I felt bad for the poor guys. All they wanted was to slather her in kisses—I knew the feeling—but all of us would have to wait for that.

"Easy," I breathed, catching her hand. "They're just checking you out."

She peeked her head up and smiled unconvincingly. "They're...*cute*."

I barked a laugh, my heart finally slowing as I collapsed flat onto my back, my feet still on the floor. "C'mere," I rumbled, giving her hand a tug.

"Are you sure they can't get out?"

"Positive. The only thing safer would be if I put the vacuum in the doorway. They're terrified of the damn thing."

"It's not the worst idea you've had, then." Still nervously staring at the door, she scooted down to lie beside me, but after the heart attack we'd both narrowly avoided for completely different reasons, she wasn't nearly close enough. She didn't argue as I dragged her against my side.

"Well, that was an eventful start to the evening," I said.

She rested her head on my shoulder and gave me a warm squeeze. "I ruined your burgers."

"The floor does seem to catch a lot of food when you're around."

She pinched my side. "No teasing me right now. I feel awful."

I pinched her right back. "Nah. We still have brats. My sister thought I'd scare you away with my burgers anyway. She claims that I can be—and I quote—'a little heavy-handed with the seasoning.'"

Her head popped up, her gaze finding mine. Color had returned to her face, but surprise was still very much present. "You told your sister about me?"

Technically yes and no.

I smoothed down the unruly blond hairs attempting to free themselves from the confines of her braids. "Is there something wrong with that?"

"Not at all." She grinned, biting her lip in a failed attempt to hide it.

"What about you? Have you told anyone about me yet?"

She crinkled her nose and grimaced. "Mark's been working a lot, so I haven't seen him much since you stopped glowering at me all the time."

I rolled my eyes. "I didn't *glower* at you."

"Fine. Smolder. Is that better?"

"Marginally."

"Aaron's usually my go-to guy for all things dating when I meet someone new. But he's been going through a lot with the settlement and all. It hasn't been the right time." Something facetious spread across her features. "Besides, despite your mouth being magnetized by mine, I'm not sure what there is to tell him yet. It's not like I know anything about *his* accounting professionals or anything. But that's neither here nor there. What'd you say to your sister?"

I relaxed deeper into the mattress. "Just that I met a woman with a foliage fetish who flashed me at the courthouse and then tried to kill me with peanut butter cookies."

"Mmm," she hummed. "So only the good stuff?"

Laughing, I tickled her side. "It's all been good stuff."

She dissolved into giggles while batting my hands away. "Bowen, stop."

Sugar let out a loud yip and we both turned to look. At the attention, he started playing pattycake with the door again.

"How long have you had them?" she asked.

"Clyde, the big one, I've had since shortly after I graduated college. I've only had Sugar for about a year though. There's still a lot of puppy in him."

"Him?" She sat all the way up and crisscrossed her legs

between us, both of her knees touching my side. "You named a boy dog *Sugar*?"

I shifted uncomfortably. Fuck. I hated the constant tiptoeing around my life. She was going to get quiet and apologize, which would make me feel like a grade-A asshole again. And hell, maybe I was. But if I wanted to keep her—and I did, desperately so—I needed to start opening up.

"He was Sally's dog."

Her eyes flared, but I had to give her credit. She was quick to cover it. "Was that your fiancée?"

Bringing us back to eye level, I sat up and used the pillows to prop myself up. With one swift push off the ground, I sent the swing gliding. "Yeah."

"That makes more sense."

I wasn't sure if she realized she did it, but her gaze flashed around the porch, a silent inspection of sorts. She didn't need to ask the question for me to know what she was thinking.

"She never lived here," I stated. "In case that's what you're wondering."

Remorse filled her eyes as they once again landed on me. "I wasn't going to pry."

"I know. But I wanted to tell you. Maybe crack the door for a minute." I willed myself to let the moment happen, to open up just enough. "Before the crash, she lived through the unimaginable, Remi. And no matter how hard I tried, I couldn't fix the world for her. I'd love to tell you more about her, but in order to do that, I'd have to tell you all the ways I'd failed her. So let's make a deal. You can ask me anything you want about Sally or the plane crash. But if I can't answer you right away, we put it on pause and come back to it when I can."

I expected her brilliant smile.

I expected her to look me in the eye and tell me none of it mattered—even though we both knew it did.

I even expected a barrage of questions she'd been mulling over all week.

But I never thought the first thing to come out of her mouth would be, "I'm not sure not being able to fix the *world* for someone counts as a failure. That's a tall order even for a man like you, Bowen."

My heart stopped as she inched closer, the crickets serenading us as the sun lazily slipped away.

"It may not have turned out the way you hoped, but—in my opinion—loving someone through, despite, and after the impossible is quite literally the definition of success in a relationship."

My chest burned as I stared into her sapphire eyes. I'd heard similar words before from my mom, my sister… Hell, even Tyson had tried his hand at the pep talk thing a time or two. But they were my family and thus required to be my biggest cheerleaders, reassuring me I'd done everything right no matter if it was the truth or not.

It was different coming from her. It meant so much more.

The constant pressure building inside me eased, as though a boulder had been removed from my chest.

This wasn't the first time Remi had given me back the ability to breathe. Her smile. Her laugh. Just the sight of her, even when I was trying to convince myself I couldn't have her, was oxygen for a man on the verge of suffocation.

And she wanted me. Why? I would never understand.

But I was also a smart enough man to know that when the

world hands you a miracle, you don't take it for granted by asking questions.

"Look." She shook her head, misreading my silence. "I don't know what happened, so please don't think I'm speaking out of turn. But—"

Snaking a hand out, I palmed the back of her head. "Stop talking."

Guilt painted her beautiful face. "Bowen, I—"

"Stop." I leaned in closer with every word. "Fucking. Talking."

Her eyes narrowed, pure Remi Grey attitude locked and loaded.

I had a better plan for her mouth.

chapter
SEVENTEEN

Remi

As only Bowen's could, his mouth came down over mine with a tender possession. How did he have such a powerful control over my body? Such a connection. Such a hold on me. I was not a prude or an angel, but if I were being honest, I hadn't been intimate—like *really* intimate—with a man in a long, long time.

Not that I was nervous about being with Bowen, because I'd never felt so drawn to someone. But also, I didn't want to get carried away physically if he wasn't ready emotionally.

It wouldn't be good for either of us. Plus, I wanted whatever this was budding between us to last. I wanted the man's body seven different ways to Sunday, but when his mouth claimed mine and his strong yet gentle hands caressed my body as we lay on the massive swing, I reminded myself again to slow down and smell the flowers.

"Wait," I whispered, cupping the side of his face.

His low voice filled my ear as he nibbled at my neck. "What are you doing to me, Remi?"

My mouth fell open as his teeth grazed the soft skin below my ear, chills exploding across my skin. "I'm making the serious, albeit probably frustrating, decision right now to slow us down so you don't do something you'll regret."

His head popped up, a scowl I hadn't seen since the bubble tea incident crinkling the space between his eyes. "Are you kidding me? The only thing I'm regretting right now is that I didn't drag you back here the day I laid eyes on you at the courthouse."

I smiled, basking in the realization that the attraction went both ways. "Are you sure? I don't want all the talk of accidents and the past to cloud the present."

He blew out a ragged breath. "Okay. That's fair. But just so you know, I don't feel the pain or the clouds of the past when we're together. Being with you is the only time I ever feel the warmth of the sun."

Emotion lodged in my throat as I stared at him.

It was different for me, but a part of me had been cold and shrouded by darkness for too long too. I hadn't understood it when I'd met him, but Bowen's own brand of warmth had been enveloping me from the very moment I laid eyes on him.

I had no hesitations when it came to being with him. No second thoughts or fears. And if he could say the same, then who was I to stop him from giving us what we both so desperately needed?

"You should probably get back to kissing me, then." I offered him a playful grin. "And maybe lose some of the clothes."

His breath caught as he stared at me, an inferno igniting in his eyes. "Do you really want this?"

It was such a simple question, and his sincerity cut me deep.

"Of course. Don't you?"

"You have no fucking clue how much I need to feel you right now." Reaching behind his head, he clutched the back of his shirt and pulled it off.

I'd been so damn wrong. His clothes had done his chiseled body absolutely no justice. His stomach was rippled, his chest carved to perfection, and even the deep V disappearing into his jeans looked as though it had been cut from stone. Unabashedly, I stared as he unbuttoned his jeans. He left them open as he toed his shoes off.

No man had any business being that sexy while removing his socks.

If I'd thought his skills at undressing himself were impressive, the scorching swiftness with which he used to strip me bare was downright masterful.

"Fuck," he groaned, sucking my nipple into his mouth.

I arched off the mattress, running my hands through his hair as he worshipped my body with his lips and hands. He was still wearing pants and I had never in my life resented something so damn much.

But to his credit, he found all the right spots. *All of them.* The place on my collarbone that made my toes curl when he licked it. The sensitive area on my hip that had me bucking into him when the slightest pressure was given by his strong hands. The way he nipped at the inside of my thigh when he removed my panties, the last stitch of fabric on my body.

He was working me over, and I'd be damned if there was

a single thing I could do to stop the flood of need that washed over me with every glance and touch.

His chest rumbled as my hand slipped into his open fly, dipping beneath a pair of black boxer briefs, and palmed his hard cock.

"That's what you do to me, Remi. You feel that? That's all for you."

"Yes," I panted before his mouth found mine again.

I gasped when his hand found my core, and together we explored each other. We pressed and ground. Took our time, not wanting to waste a single sensation.

Soon, I'd inched the denim and his briefs down his hips and my hand stretched to close around his thickness. I was wanton and desperate as he gently circled my clit exactly the way I liked it.

I was either going to die or roll him over and take what I needed. Much more of his skilled attention and my money was on the latter.

"Please," I begged. "More."

His glassy eyes met mine as he rose above me, his hand leaving my center. Then, as if I weren't already putty in his hands, he brought his talented fingers to his mouth and sucked my wetness from the tips.

"Mmm, heaven," he whispered.

A whimper tumbled from my lips, but he didn't stop there.

His finger left his mouth, and without hesitation, he held my gaze as he guided his length to my entrance and pushed inside, seating himself at the hilt.

"Fuck," he rasped. "This is mine. Do you hear me? Nobody else's."

As charity would have it, I didn't mind belonging to him, so I agreed. "All yours."

I'd needed that.

That possession.

That owning.

It had been missing in my life for as long as I could remember. But there in that moment, I realized nothing before that night even mattered.

I was his, and as he began a relentless rhythm inside me, he showed me exactly what that meant.

It was feral and passionate.

It was pawing and scratching.

It was holding my breath when I didn't know how much more I could take before my limbs flew away with the wind and my body shattered into fragments of desire and flesh.

It was the way his back flexed under my palms as he drove into me and how he rolled to his back, never breaking our connection, so I could ride out my pleasure, straddling the gorgeous man I'd been lucky enough to find in the unlikeliest of places.

It was crying his name as he devoured my body until I thought the sun would come up and reveal that it had all been just a dream.

But it wasn't.

It was real.

And the notion that Bowen could truly be mine left me higher than any orgasm ever could.

"Fuck me," he whispered as he collapsed beside me, dragging me over to lie at his side when he flipped to his back.

I nuzzled into the curve of his neck. "I believe that's what I just did."

He hummed and kissed the top of my head. "I could do this all night."

For a second, I considered starving and catching the play-by-play highlights on SportsCenter later, but knowing better, I tipped my head back to look at him. "All night? You might need some nourishment if you plan to last that long."

A breathy chuckle rumbled at my cheek. "Oh, ye of little faith."

"No, ye had little lunch. Ye needs meat and maybe a beer or two."

Right on cue, my tummy growled, and without missing a beat, he slid down my side and pressed his ear to my stomach.

"What was that?" He shifted and kissed my sensitive skin, and then he went back to listening as I held in a giggle. My insides answered him. "Oh, really? Well, we can't have that. I'm not the only one who's going to need to last all night. I mean, I am a master at flying solo, but—"

Clearing my throat, I interrupted. "I don't mean to break up this very cute thing you have going on right now with my digestive tract, but I need to get cleaned up and you need to feed me dinner. We have a game to watch."

His eyes turned dark and both corners of his mouth twitched. "Or I could just stay down here and have you for dinner."

Sweet Lord have mercy. It was tempting.

I sat up far enough to catch his face, press a kiss to his forehead, and then I suggested in my most convincing tone a better solution. "Or maybe you feed me and then have me for dessert."

"You drive a hard bargain," he relented as he rose, naked and outrageously gorgeous.

I offered him not a lick of privacy as he bent to grab his pants from the ground. My gaze ate him up one inch at a time.

His abs rippled as he stepped into each leg and tugged them up over his gloriously hard ass. Focusing on the button of his jeans, he said, "You keep looking at me like that and, instead of feeding you, we're going to be testing the payload of the bolts I used to hang that damn swing again."

"What? It's not my fault. I feel certain the other nerds do not know you are working with *that*." I circled my finger in the air, pointing to the bulge tenting the front of his pants. Clearly, I was the only one not quite ready for round two.

A devilish smile played at his lips. "I'll go lock the dogs up. Give me two minutes and you can come in and get cleaned up." He found the remote beside me and tossed it onto my lap. "Put the game on."

Neither of us wasted any time. In a matter of about twenty minutes, we were eating the most flavorful brats and loaded baked potatoes while slugging back beers as Boston showed our bullpen who was boss.

I didn't even care.

The game was a lost cause by the time he took my plate and empty bottle inside with his and returned looking hungrier than before we'd eaten. He kissed up and down my neck while I typed out a quick message to Aaron, letting him know I wouldn't be home, using some lame excuse about having a girls' night out with Amber and some of her college friends. He'd see right through it, but at least he wouldn't worry until I could fill him in on all things Bowen Michaels.

"You ready to go inside? I'll give you the grand tour of the bedroom," Bowen asked, nipping at my ear.

"Mmm," I hummed, threading my fingers into the top of his hair. "Maybe."

"Maybe? What else could you possibly need right now?" He grinned. "Water?" After clicking the TV off, he sat up, shoved an arm under my legs, and scooped me up in one fluid movement. "An after-dinner mint?" Barefooted, he cocked an eyebrow and carried me inside the house. "Does my clumsy girl need to stretch first?"

I laughed and rested my head against his chest, his thin, dark hair tickling my cheek. "I'm good."

He smiled wolfishly. "I think I can make you better."

And dear God, better was exactly what he gave me. For hours, he worked my body, alternating between worshipping me and driving me to the point of insanity. By the time it was all said and done, there wasn't a part of my body he hadn't touched—or that I wouldn't spend the entirety of the night hoping he'd touch again. I was going to be exhausted at work the next day, but that was a small price to pay when he curled behind me, cocooning me in the safety of his arms.

Falling asleep, sore, sated, and breathless, I felt something new in my heart. Something peaceful and complete.

Bowen Michaels might have thought he'd failed at love before, but he was healing me with it now.

chapter
EIGHTEEN

Remi

"Nice job," my physical therapist, John, praised as I collapsed flat onto the mat.

Cradling my shoulder, I mumbled, "Didn't feel nice."

He laughed and nudged me with the toe of his sneaker. "Maybe not now, but you'll thank me one day. You're only stuck with me for a few more weeks, right?"

"Yep. I'm counting down the days. Not that I don't enjoy your company. It's just..." I gingerly sat up and curled my tired arms to my chest. They felt like noodles that had been cooked too long. "Nope. I lied. That's exactly what it is."

He barked a laugh and walked toward his next client, calling out, "Ah, quit your complaining. I'll see you next week."

I groaned at the thought. Before the crash, I had been no stranger to the gym. Though I had always been more of a cardio girl with the occasional weights thrown in. I still ran when

the difference between SOMEBODY and SOMEONE

I had the chance, but after I'd spent eight weeks with both arms in casts, physical therapy was a different kind of beast altogether.

"You looked good today," Ms. Linda said, standing over me, extending a water bottle in my direction. In her mid-sixties, she was something of the grandmother at Atlanta PT. Though she didn't look like any grandmother I knew. Tall and lean, with thick, rich auburn hair and gorgeous green eyes, she was easily one of my favorite people at the physical therapy center—though John didn't exactly give her much competition.

During our many chats, I'd learned she was a retired nurse who had taken to volunteering a few months earlier. She mostly walked around telling everyone how awesome they were doing while handing out water, sports drinks, and on more than one occasion homecooked brownies. Not to brag, but also to brag, it was a well-known fact that I was her favorite.

"Thanks," I said, taking the water bottle and making quick work of twisting off the cap and lifting it for a long drink.

"No problem at all, kiddo." She walked over to a stack of mats against the wall and hoisted herself to sit on top. "Seeing you each week is always a good reminder for me to take a break. Oh, that reminds me. Next week, I'm making another batch of those chocolate drizzle Rice Krispies Treats. Would you like me to bring you another pan?"

See? Totally her favorite.

I arched an admonishing eyebrow. "Are you going to let me pay you this time?"

"Sure," she chirped.

"Wait. Let me rephrase. Are you going to let me pay you this time and not sneak it back into my purse on my way out?"

"Oh, then, no." She winked. "You want 'em or not?"

I groaned as I pushed up to my feet. "Of course I want them, Linda. Nobody in their right mind says no to your culinary perfection."

"Just for that, you're getting extra chocolate drizzle."

And just for *that*, I was going to have to get creative when it came to hiding money in her back pocket like a reverse robbery. I had her phone number. Surely she had a Venmo or something set up.

"You're too good to me." I stretched my hands above my head and leaned from side to side. As much as I hated to admit it, John was right. I always felt a little stronger the next day.

She smiled. "I try."

I walked over to my bag and picked my phone up. Aaron had already texted me three times asking me if I was on my way yet. It could be said I didn't have the most punctual track record when it came to our weekly coffee dates—or in general. But today, I had an entire weekend of Bowen Michaels to fill him in on and only an hour between his meetings. I couldn't afford to be late. I still wasn't positive the timing was right to tell him, but after I'd stayed the night at Bowen's, I wasn't sure how much longer I could keep putting it off.

I typed out a quick *On my way* and then started collecting my stuff.

"I have to head out. But next week, it's me, you, a pan of Rice Krispies Treats with extra chocolate drizzle, and forty bucks, right?"

She shook her head. "Get out of here with that nonsense."

the difference between **SOMEBODY** and **SOMEONE**

I hooked my bag over my shoulder. "Okay, okay, fine. *Fifty bucks.*"

She rolled her eyes and shooed me with her hands. "You better stop before I change my mind."

I squeaked at the threat she would never follow through with and zipped my lips closed. With one last grin, I jogged to the door.

"Later, Remi!" John called from across the gym.

I lifted two fingers in a peace sign before busting out of there.

It wasn't a long drive, but I was still ten minutes late. The expression on Aaron's sourpuss face when I walked into the café made it seem like I'd left him there for the better part of a decade.

He glared at me as I hurried over in a pair of yoga pants and an off-the-shoulder cropped sweatshirt I'd thrown on over my tank top. I sank down into the chair across from him and focused on his forehead. "You do know that's the face that causes those wrinkles you've been bitching about."

His eyes flashed wide, and he rubbed his fingers across his forehead. "So it's your fault I suddenly look a hundred years old."

I lifted the latte he'd bought me and clicked my paper cup with his. "I plead the Fifth."

He moved his fingertips to his nonexistent crow's feet. "Does the Fifth cover my antiaging cream?"

"Psh. Don't act like you don't already use mine."

That finally earned me a smile, even if he looked away so I wouldn't see it.

"Don't be mad," I said. "I really did leave when I texted

you. I got a call while I was in the parking lot. I'm sorry for making you wait."

His gaze came back to mine, a brilliant white smile splitting his mouth. "It's fine. I'm just giving you shit." He leaned in close. "The hot barista gave me her number."

I couldn't help it. I immediately flicked my gaze to the counter.

"Stop looking," he hissed.

Which honestly is the worst possible thing you can say to a person in that situation. Because it made me look back at him before my brain forced my gaze back to her. And when her eyes made contact with mine mid-visual seizure, I made it even worse by squinting and staring up at the menu over her head as if I didn't already have a drink in front of me.

There was no way to deny we were talking about her.

"Sweet Jesus," Aaron muttered, going back to rubbing his forehead. "Anyway, heads up, I told her I was meeting my *sister* here so she wouldn't get the wrong idea when you arrived. Not that it matters anymore."

A laugh bubbled from my throat, and as much as he probably wanted to strangle me, he laughed too.

"I hope you're planning on living with me forever because, at this rate, that's how long I'll be single." He brought his coffee to his lips.

"That's actually why I wanted to meet up for coffee today. I kinda sorta met someone too."

Cupping his ear with his hand, he blinked rapidly. "I'm sorry, what?"

"So, um, you remember Mr. Tall, Dark, and Nice Ass who gave me the safety pin?"

His back shot straight and his neck snapped back. "At the courthouse?"

"That's the one."

He leaned back in his chair, crossing his leg ankle to knee, only to shift in his chair to do the same on the other side. "Care to elaborate on that?"

"Well, his name is Bowen. He's six-four, nerdy and broody at the same time, and quite literally the sexiest man I've ever laid eyes on."

Aaron snapped his fingers. "I've seen him. Get to the good stuff. Did he ask you out the day of the settlement hearing? How long have you been seeing him? And why the hell haven't you told me until now?"

"You've had a lot going on," I defended. "I didn't want to be all hearts and rainbows while you were dealing with doom and gloom."

He huffed, knowing I had a point, and twirled two fingers in the air. "And what about the rest of it? Is he who you were with last night while you were lying to me about a girls' night out with your imaginary girlfriends?"

"If you must know..." I rested my elbows on the table, partitioned off my mouth as though anyone else in the empty coffee shop were paying us attention, and whispered, "Yes, I was out with Bowen having the best sex of my entire life. I'm talking multiple orgasms from a man with a huge cock who didn't need an instructional video on how to find my clit. And I swear, if you give me one single ounce of shit about it, I'm going to launch myself over this table in front of Sexy Barista Lady and rain down hell over you for not sending child support for our brother-cousin children."

His jaw hung open, and it was almost a shame I didn't know exactly what part of that verbal tornado had packed the biggest punch.

Leaning back, I mirrored his position and casually took a sip of my coffee. "But to answer your original question, no, he didn't ask me out at the courthouse. I Googled him, found out he was an accountant, showed up at his office, spilled bubble tea all over his waiting room, and then asked him to help me with my father's taxes. When he'd finally agreed, I promptly charmed the pants off him by learning how to use his EpiPen." I primped my hair even though it was currently in a messy ponytail.

How, after all these years, Aaron still found himself speechless, I would never understand. That didn't make the sight of his bulging eyes and gaping mouth any less entertaining.

His lids fell shut and he drew in a sharp breath. But he held it in as he waved his hand in front of his face. "First, please never say clit again. I beg you. I'm completely content with the assumption that you have the anatomy of a Barbie Doll. Do not ruin that for me." His eyes finally opened, a confusing amount of concern crinkling his forehead. Damn, I *would* have to buy him his own face cream after this. "Second—and let me get this straight—you elbowed this man in the face, stalked him down, asked him to be your accountant, and then had sex with him?"

I chewed on the inside of my cheek. "You make it sound so aggressive. Let's try this version: My cursed dress broke and he saved the day with a safety pin. Then a few days later, when I saw him inside a pub, I stopped to say thank you. There was a lot of frowning and debate about my plant budget. But he ended up buying me and Margret a drink anyway."

"Margret?"

"A plant."

"*Another one?*"

"Anyway... Then I looked him up, gave him back the safety pin, to which he decided to stalk *me* down and give me a cactus. Then we did the accounting stuff, and as of last night...the sex stuff too. Better?"

He put his elbows on the table and steepled his fingers in front of his mouth. "And you like him?"

"Oh my God, Aaron. So, so much. When he's not being all mercurial and obtuse, he's sweet and funny—even when he's not trying to be. And when he looks at me..." I let out a soft moan. "I don't know how to describe it. It's like the entire world vanishes. I don't care if it's cheesy. I've never felt like this before."

His jaw flexed and he squinted as he mulled it over. "You can't say that. You've known him, what? All of two weeks?"

"Yep. Funny enough, most of that time, he didn't even want to give me the time of day. But I am telling you, there is something about him I can't shake. It's something big. Huge, even."

He winced, lifting a hand to stop me, probably assuming I was headed back to the topic of sex, but this thing between me and Bowen was so much more than that.

"You know, I've never said this before, and if things fizzle out, I will eat every single one of these words. But I really think I could fall in love with him."

"Christ," he whispered, scrubbing his thumb and forefinger over his eyes. "You're serious about this?"

"I am."

"And it doesn't concern you that he's a survivor who is going to come with his own load of baggage?"

"Oh, come on, Aaron. You and I have enough issues to fill this coffee shop ten times over. Are we really judging people because of them now?"

He stared at me for several silent beats, something I couldn't quite figure out passing through his features. "I just want things to be easy for you for once."

"I don't want easy. I want passion and fire, spontaneity and security. So what if he's a survivor? There are exactly twenty-six other people who truly understand the situation we've been through. And considering I don't even have a vagina as far as you're concerned, my dating pool is down to twenty-five. But honestly, it could be ten thousand and I'd still want him."

He blew out a controlled breath. "All right."

"Really?"

"Don't act so surprised. I don't care who he is as long as he makes you happy. Though you should hold off on telling Mark for a while. He and that bartender just broke up." He took a sip of coffee.

My head snapped back. "What bartender?"

"It seems I'm the only one without a secret lover these days."

"Wait, wait, wait. He's been seeing someone and didn't tell me? What the hell?"

Aaron scowled. "Oh, look, it's little Miss Hypocrisy."

the difference between SOMEBODY and SOMEONE

I rolled my eyes. "Who is she? And how did you find out before me? What did he even wear when they went out? I've dressed him for every date he's been on since high school."

Using the back of his fingers, he brushed off the shoulder of the tan slim-fit sweater Mark would have rather thrown himself off a bridge than put on. "Curious, isn't it? He's been single all this time."

"Oh, hush. Spill the deets."

"No." He laughed. "What kind of friend would that make me? And you just give this thing with Bowen some time and see where it goes. If it fizzles, then there's nothing to tell Mark anyway. If it turns into something more permanent, Mark will be happy for you too. But maybe figure it out before you pour salt in his wound."

I pursed my lips. Omission because I hadn't seen him recently was one thing, but I hated the idea of flat-out lying to him long term. But then again, the few times Mark had been in a relationship, they'd always ended with him being shredded. He was a big guy with a big heart; when it was ripped out, the gaping hole left behind was massive.

"Hold up. Was it one of *his* bartenders? He has to know better than to date someone who works for him. Right?"

Aaron shook his head. "Just leave it alone."

"You suck."

He smirked. "I can live with…" The bell over the door rang, and Aaron's words trailed off as his eyes grew wide.

I didn't have to look to know who'd walked in. He'd called me as I'd pulled into the parking lot to see if I wanted to join him for an early lunch. I had. Absolutely. I also wanted to introduce him to my best friend. So I'd told him to meet me at the café five minutes before Aaron had to leave.

"Be nice," I whispered to Aaron before turning in my chair. The minute Bowen's eyes found mine, a devastating smile curled his lips.

I walked over to meet him, and he did not delay in pulling me in for a hug. The scruff on his jaw brushed my cheek, sending a chill down my spine as I remembered what it felt like on the inside of my thighs.

He put his lips to my ear and whispered, "Why do I feel like I just crashed a party?"

"It's fine. You're just early." I tilted my head back, puckering my lips, ready and waiting for his signature greeting, but his mouth never made it to mine. He was too busy staring at Aaron over my shoulder.

"You told me you wanted me to meet your friend, so I came right away."

I pressed up onto my toes and stole a peck. "Come on. I'll introduce you."

Like a gentleman, Aaron stood up when we reached the table.

Unlike a gentleman, he stood there without so much as a hello.

"Bowen, this is Aaron Lanier, my best friend. Aaron, this is Bowen Michaels, my..." I twisted my lips, unsure how to finish that thought.

Bowen, on the other hand, was not. Hooking an arm around my hips, he pulled me against his side. "Her man."

Her man? Um, yes please.

My body hummed, a fire igniting inside me. Fuck. Now

was not the time to throw the man—*my* man—to the ground and mount him.

"Nice to meet you," Aaron said, finally extending a hand to Bowen.

Bowen cupped it firmly. "You too. I've heard a lot of good things."

Aaron's gaze slid to mine. "As of about ten minutes ago, so have I."

"In that case, my timing seems impeccable."

"It appears so," Aaron mumbled, dropping his hand and settling back into his seat.

Bowen grabbed a chair from the table beside ours and dragged it over, sliding it so close to mine they touched. Once seated, he slid his arm across the back of my chair. "So, what do you do for a living, Aaron?"

"Computer engineering at Rubicon."

Bowen's eyes perked. "The body armor company?"

Aaron fidgeted with his coffee cup. "Yep."

"Very nice."

"Yep," Aaron repeated.

My shoulders sagged as a wet blanket of silence fell over the table. Okay, so this was not the bellows of laughter, instant connection, and planning future vacations together I'd hoped for when introducing two of my favorite guys. But it wasn't *bad*, either. Aaron could be slow to warm up sometimes, and Bowen, well… I had no idea what he was like around new people. If the initial situation I'd had with him was anything to go by, Aaron would be the proud recipient of a cactus sometime next week.

"Hey." I looked at Bowen. "Can I grab you a coffee?"

"Thanks, but I can get it, babe."

"No, I don't mind." I stood up and put a hand on each of their shoulders. Both were wound like a rubber band ready to snap. "It will give you guys a few minutes to get to know each other better." I cut Bowen a teasing side-eye. "Let me guess. Americano black?"

He pitched his lips to the side. "Close. Milk. Two Splendas."

"Right. That was my second guess."

Bowen smiled and Aaron just sat there, his face unreadable, like a true conversationalist.

Awesome.

Shaking my head, I walked to the counter, hoping like hell I didn't come back to find them both scrolling on their phones.

"Hi. What can I get you?" the barista asked with a gorgeous white smile. I hoped to God Aaron had already secured a date because there was no way this woman didn't have a stack of applications waiting in her inbox.

I placed my order and desperately fought the urge to put in a good word for my friend. After at least a dozen failed blind dates, he hated when I meddled in his love life, and I was already needling his patience with this ambush.

It didn't take but a few minutes for her to pour the coffee, and after a pit stop at the cream and sugar bar, I was on my way back to the table.

Much to my absolute delight, the guys were hunched forward and talking when I approached, but my glee was short-lived.

Aaron's hand was balled into a fist, resting on the wooden

top between them. "...because I will fucking kill you. Do you understand me? And I'm not even the one you need to be worried about. If Mark—"

"Hey!" I scolded, setting Bowen's cup on the table. "Seriously? I walk away for two minutes and you're issuing death threats?"

Aaron clamped his mouth shut and had the good sense to look sheepish.

Bowen chuckled, momentarily stealing my outrage. "Remi, it's okay. Cut the man some slack. He's your best friend. It's his duty to threaten my life if I were to hurt you. I'd be disappointed if he didn't."

"Well, that's just..." I flicked my gaze between the two of them. A brawl didn't seem likely, though I had wrestled Aaron to the floor over the remote a time or two, so I was fairly confident Bowen could hold his own. "Unnecessary."

He reached out and caught my hand, pulling me back onto my chair. "And that is exactly what I was about to tell him." Grinning, he returned his attention to Aaron. "You have nothing to worry about. I assure you I have Remi's best interest at the forefront of my every thought. No consequence you could ever issue me would be worse than the hell I would suffer if she got hurt—in any way."

"Awww." I tilted my head back and peered up at him. Okay, so it was seriously sweet. Still wildly unnecessary. But sweet nonetheless.

He shot me a wink and looked back at Aaron. "So, how do you feel about baseball? Remi and I talked about catching a home game sometime. We'd love it if you'd join us."

I slapped a hand over my mouth. He might as well have offered Aaron a root canal.

Aaron frowned. "So very tempting, but I'm sure I have to work."

"Weekend night game?" Bowen offered, the side of his mouth twitching.

"Especially then." Aaron glanced at his watch and then pushed to his feet. "Speaking of, I should probably get back to the office."

Bowen immediately stood and extended a hand. "Well, it was great to meet you."

"Yeah," Aaron mumbled. "You too. I'll see you at home, Remi." He slanted his head. "Or is tonight another girls' night out?"

Bowen grinned and gave my hand a pointed squeeze. We didn't have plans, but I was certainly more than willing to make some.

"I'll let you know."

With that, Aaron put his hand out as he walked past, and I slapped it in a low five. He went straight to the counter, whispered something to the barista that made her giggle, and then headed out the door with nothing but swagger in his step.

My eyes darted to Bowen. "Well, that could have gone better."

He finally took a sip of his coffee. "What are you talking about? I thought it went great. He's a nice guy who obviously cares about you a lot. I automatically like him."

"Good, because death threats aside, he's the best."

"I have no doubt he is." He dipped his head and pressed a kiss to my lips. "Now let's talk about this girls' night. You want to do dinner after work then head back to my place for a movie? I'm not great at nail polish or face masks, but I make killer popcorn." He kissed the back of my hand and then lowered it to his lap, hidden by the table. Resting my hand right on top of his cock.

My eyes flashed wide, and I bit the inside of my cheek. Not the least bit scandalized, but thoroughly turned on. And just because the torture could not be limited to me, I traced my thumb up his thickening length.

"Easy," he rumbled.

I leaned in close enough for my breath to whisper over his ear. "Or we could skip dinner and order takeout?" Using my palm, I gave his cock as much of a stroke as his slacks would allow.

He caught my wrist, his heated gaze holding mine. "Chinese it is. Pack an overnight bag."

chapter
NINETEEN

Bowen

"Yes," she breathed, hunched over in the shower. Her soft curves were pinned to my front, hot water cascading down around us, my fingers playing between her legs, teasing her clit. "Bowen!" she gasped, reaching up to grip the back of my neck.

She was about to come again. I could feel it building, her muscles tightening, her legs shaking. She was barely even breathing anymore. At this point, I could write an entire fucking manual on how to make this woman come.

It had been a long night of lovemaking. We'd started with a picnic of moo shu chicken laid out across the coffee table, but my main course was a very naked and wet Remi Grey.

My body ached. Muscles I hadn't known I had screamed from overuse. And we both had to get showered, dressed, properly caffeinated, and then off to work.

Still, I wanted more.

"Wider," I ordered, nudging the inside of her thighs with my hand.

I couldn't get enough of her, and only part of that had to do with her body. Though I couldn't keep track of how many times I'd gotten her off, my number was significantly lower, but only because biology was a merciless son of a bitch.

She must have been sore, but she stepped to the side and opened her body for me yet again. Insatiable.

So much for getting cleaned up before breakfast.

I drove into her from behind with devastating control. Her beautiful round ass pressed against my hips as I bottomed out inside her.

"Oh, God, yes," she moaned, folding over and slapping her hand against the wall for balance.

I worked her slow and gentle, sliding a hand up the delicate curve of her back before curling it around to cup her breast. Her echoing moans were a symphony as I started a rhythm of deep thrusts.

She stepped over the edge first, her tight heat milking the orgasm from my cock.

How I remained upright would forever be a mystery, but as I came with her name torn from my throat, I folded over on top of her. Panting and spent, my thighs on fire, I rested my head between her shoulder blades.

"You have got to stop seducing me," I rasped.

"You're right. I never should have asked you to pass the shampoo. How very thoughtless and manipulative of me."

Barely finding the energy to grin, I eased out of her and stood up straight.

She turned into me, bringing her arms up between us to

cuddle against my front, edging me out of the stream of hot water altogether.

"Is it going to set you ablaze again if I ask for the loofa?"

"Possibly. Though my cock is going to need an ICU bed if we try that again."

She smiled and a tidal wave of pure sated happiness hit my chest.

It was something so simple for most people. But in my world, smiles were not a given any more than waking up next to the same woman I'd fallen asleep beside. And when it had come to Sally, convincing her that life was worth waking up for in general had been a constant struggle.

Eventually, I'd annoy Remi. She'd annoy me. We'd bicker and argue. Hell, we might not even talk for a few days while emotions calmed. We were human. Bad days were a given.

But not having to spend the bad days in a state of paralyzed terror, unsure if the good ones existed anymore, was a dream I never knew I could have again.

Yet there I stood with Remi's blue eyes locked with mine. Her hair wet and her lips swollen. A smile that could ease even the most tormented soul aimed up at me. With that, the bad days didn't just seem bearable. I was fucking eager for the innate monotony of something so blissfully normal.

She was happy, serenely so.

And I was falling in love with the possibility that my current reality was far better than the haunting and hypothetical what-could-have-beens of the past.

Lowering my head, I sealed my mouth over hers in a languid kiss.

"Mmm," she hummed. Looping her arms around my neck,

she leaned away, her life-altering smile never fading. "You should know that I spent way too much time in the hospital to go back. So, if you put the moves on me again, I will be waiting until your cock gets out of the ICU before paying it another visit."

I released her instantly. "Whoa. No need to talk crazy. Let me get some soap and hot water and I'll get out to make breakfast."

She squeezed a dollop of bodywash into my hand. "Oh, please. With that last little stunt of yours, we're too late for breakfast even by my standards."

"Your confidence in me is insulting." I did the world's fastest lather-and-rinse routine and then slapped her on the ass—not hard enough to leave a mark, but definitely enough to cause my cock to stir back to life.

Fuck. I could not get enough of the woman.

While she finished up in the bathroom, I let the dogs out of the guest room. I didn't think they were as fond of having her over as I was, but with a little time, I had no doubt she'd come around to loving them. I gave it a few weeks before she would be cuddling with Sugar on the couch, maybe a month for Clyde.

I was still getting dressed when I heard the shower turn off. It was safer for both of us if I tied my tie and fastened my cuff links in the kitchen and not in a room with a bed where I ran the risk of her dropping her towel.

By the time she finally emerged from my room, she was wearing a sophisticated little black dress that clung to her every curve and a pair of red sky-high heels. Her hair was pulled up into a high ponytail, the curls still slightly damp, and her makeup was minimal but no less drop-dead sexy.

I let out a low whistle. "Jesus, woman. You look incredible.

Please tell me your closing this morning is with two ogres and a blind man."

She narrowed her eyes. "Do I sense a hint of jealousy?"

I prowled toward her, sliding my palms up her sides, not stopping as my thumbs brushed the curve of her breasts. "I'm jealous of anyone who gets to spend the morning with you. Ogre or not."

She grabbed both of my wrists and forced my arms back to my sides. "Oh, no. You are not starting that again, Mister Suave. No touching. Some people actually have to get to work." She sniffed the air. "Speaking of, what happened to breakfast?"

Reluctantly, though necessary, I dragged two bowls toward us on the bar. "No time to cook, but I made travel mugs of coffee and"—I turned, grabbing the box from the cabinet and then placing it on the counter in front of her—"homemade, from scratch, breakfast of successful and productive adults everywhere."

She drew in a sharp breath, her mouth stretching into a bright white smile that I swear warmed the entire room.

Fuck me, the woman was going to be the end of me and I was an all-too-willing victim.

"Frosted Flakes are my favorite!" She picked up the box and turned it in her hands. "I pegged you all wrong, Michaels. I figured, with two Splendas in your coffee and a set of abs that won't quit, you'd be a Raisin Bran kind of guy."

My mouth fell open in feigned injury as I reached back into the cabinet. "I'm offended." I pulled down a box of Raisin Bran and dropped it onto the counter with a loud thud. "And also thoroughly impressed."

"I knew it!"

While she dissolved into a fit of laughter, I opened the brand-new box of Frosted Flakes and filled her bowl. "You knew nothing. So what, I like to eat healthy during the week so I can keep up with a certain ravenous woman but then also treat myself with roughly a pound of sugar per bowl on the weekend. What of it?"

She laughed again as I poured in the milk and then slid breakfast her way. "I better be that certain ravenous woman."

"Look who's jealous now," I teased, propping my hip against the counter.

She took a bite and chewed, and I stood there, eagerly awaiting her snappy reply.

"It's me. I'm jealous. I'm not sure my heart is up for sharing you."

"Then don't," I stated matter-of-factly, all the while trying to play it cool. The idea of sharing her was enough to set fire to my veins. "I sure as hell don't want anyone else."

Her cheeks pinked and she raked her teeth over her bottom lip. "Me either."

I curled my hand around the back of her neck and tipped her head. She beamed up at me, and fuck, she owned me. "Then that's settled. Nobody else exists."

"That easy, huh? Every other woman in the world just suddenly disappeared?"

I dipped down, brushing my nose with hers, her exhales filling my lungs with more life than I'd felt in God only knew how long. "There are two types of people in the world, Remi. There are a million *somebodies* on this planet. But there's a huge difference between *somebody* and *someone*. From the moment we met, I knew you, my beautiful, crazy woman, were definitely some*one*. And if there is even a fraction of a chance that you think I'm a someone too, then yeah, it's exactly that easy. To hell with the rest of the women in the world. I want you."

Tears sparkled in her eyes, and she circled her arms around my hips, hugging me tight. "Of course I think you're someone. If you want the truth, a part of me thinks you're the *only* one. But isn't this all too fast? You've been through so much and—"

"Period," I stated.

Her brows sank together, confusion contorting her beautiful face. "What?"

"You said I've been through so much. That should be the end of the statement. No *and* or continuation of thought. No one knows better than me that the last few months—hell, years—haven't been the easiest. But when I'm with you, Remi, none of it matters."

Curling my hand around the side of her face, I brushed her jaw with the pad of my thumb. "I want to explore things with you. And I mean more than just that sexy body of yours. Remi, baby, if this is just the start, imagine how good it could get." I smirked and then nipped at her bottom lip. "And if I could do that without having to wage war against every man who no doubt falls at your feet on a damn near daily basis, then no. It's not too fast. It's about fucking time."

I didn't wait for her reply.

I kissed her.

Really *kissed* her.

Tasting and exploring her mouth as if it were the very first time, because in a lot of ways, it was. It was a fresh start. The beginning. The end. Everything all rolled into one.

And fuck me, fucking fuck me, I had never been so damn excited about something in my entire life.

We were both late that morning. And not because I'd hauled her back to the bedroom the way I so desperately wanted. We sat side by side at my bar, her enjoying a bowl of Frosted Flakes, me with Raisin Bran, and toasted our new relationship with travel mugs of coffee.

We laughed.

I anchored my hand to her thigh.

And she wiped a dribble of milk off my chin with her thumb.

It was all so easy and perfectly normal.

That should have been my first sign that everything was about to go to hell all over again.

chapter TWENTY

Bowen

Remi: Good morning, boyfriend. Or are we too old for that? Manfriend? We really should iron out these titles sooner rather than later.

Me: Since you insisted on going home last night and are texting me and not lying beside me naked, there is officially nothing good about this morning.

Remi: Could you be more dramatic? It was one night. I left your house like twelve hours ago.

After unplugging my phone from the charger, I rolled over in bed, coming nose to nose with a pair of innocent doe eyes, his head on the pillow, his body tucked under the covers. As if I'd needed validation on how much it sucked waking up without Remi, he sneezed in my face.

"Jesus, Sugar." Using the back of my hand, I wiped my cheek. At the sound of my voice, Clyde took that as his cue to unfurl from his dog bed in the corner and lumber over to poke me in the back with his nose until I flipped over to share the attention.

"Okay, okay. I'm getting up."

While I'd hated my first night away from Remi that week, the dogs were pretty stoked to be allowed in the bedroom again. After a few quick head scratches, I sat up and typed another message while the dogs performed the morning ritual of trotting around the room, celebrating that I'd once again been resurrected from the dead.

Me: Twelve hours is too long.

Remi: I agree, but Aaron put tap water in the humidifiers the other night. If I don't get things straight around here, Margret is going to be as dead as you already think she is.

Me: Fine. But pack a bag for tonight. One for Margret too if that's what it takes. Bring a whole fucking rainforest. I don't give a shit.

Remi: Yes, sir.

Me: Mmm...that sounds better than both boyfriend and manfriend.

Remi: Sirfriend? How very regal of you.

Me: Don't you forget it either. I'll have a placard for my office door ordered by lunch. Sirfriend Bowen Michaels, CPA. Sounds about right.

Remi: The nerds will have to change your name in all their phones. But as long as we're picking our own titles, I'd like to be Madame Remi, Queen of Auto-Injected Epinephrine and Certified Plant Whisperer.

Me: You be at my house early today and I'll call you whatever you want.

Remi: How early? What time will you be off?

Me: Technically, I won't get off until you get here, but I have the entire day blocked out to finish your dad's stuff. I should be done by two, but I need to hit the grocery store. We're gonna try round two of burgers tonight. Be here as soon as you can swing it. We can spend the rest of the afternoon in bed making up for last night, and only then will I feed your loud, rumbly stomach. After that, it's whatever your heart desires this evening. Though I'd like to put in a formal request that, whatever it is, we do it naked too.

Remi: So…bed, food, naked fun. Got it. Well, I'm meeting a new client this morning to show him houses. He's a single guy and I found one in his price range with a theater room, so I don't expect it to last long. I should be done by three.

the difference between SOMEBODY and SOMEONE

Me: Okay. Then it's a date, Queen Mouthy.

Remi: The *Mouth* Queen. Perfect! I'll show you all my oral…I mean…royal skills this afternoon. See ya in bed at three, Sirfriend.

She was full of it. She'd see me fifteen minutes late, but knowing I'd be seeing her at all had me climbing out of my sheets with a huge grin on my face. I'd barely made it to the bathroom before my phone vibrated in my hand again.

Remi: In case you didn't notice, I missed you too. See you tonight.

It was something so simple, yet it hit me so damn deep. I swear, after months of walking around hollow-chested with a permanent chill, a little fucking sunshine in my life went a long way.

The day was relatively uneventful, but I stayed busy enough that time didn't crawl at a snail's pace. Good news was Remi's dad wouldn't be going to jail. Bad news was he owed a nice chunk of change to the IRS. So I'd set him up with a payment plan that, based on The Wave's revenue, shouldn't be an issue.

On my way home, I stopped at a plant shop before heading to the grocery store. I must have sorted through a dozen shrubs before deciding on a snake plant. It was nothing fancy or big, and it sure as hell didn't cost more than my mortgage. But with green paddle-like leaves, it was sturdy and thick.

Sure, it was technically a gift for Remi, but if she was leaving me to go home to take care of her *babies*, I sure as hell could give her something to care for at my place as well. I chose a deep-red-and-gray ceramic pot that matched my living room, and as soon as I got home, I placed it prominently on the end table. Cassidy would have something to say about me moving her precious woven basket of useless wooden balls, but she'd get over it.

The look on Remi's face would be worth whatever bullshit my sister doled out.

While I waited for her to arrive, I prepped the burgers and all the accoutrements and put them in the fridge to maximize my time with her once she inevitably got there late. I didn't think much about it when three-thirty rolled around. I made myself busy, tidying the patio and rearranging the pillows on the swing outside while throwing the ball for the dogs in an attempt to tire them out.

Then four o'clock came and I sent her a teasing text asking if her client was giving her the run around.

It came with no response. Not even a text bubble bouncing at the bottom of the screen from a text message accidentally left unsent. And I knew that because I sat and stared at the message for over an hour, a sour unease settling in my gut.

At five o'clock, it started raining. And not just a drizzle or a spring shower. It was as though the bottom had dropped out of the sky. That was when I officially gave up playing it cool and started calling her. First her cell phone, then her office. It was entirely possible she was still with a client. But the trauma inside me launched my mind into every single worst-case scenario.

I didn't even know who the hell this client was.

What if it was *him*?

What if he'd hurt her?

What if she needed me?

the difference between SOMEBODY and SOMEONE

What if I failed the woman of my dreams—again?

Deep down, I knew that it wasn't rational. She was habitually late, and it had only been two hours. But nothing about my life was rational.

I lived in the impossible. The unimaginable. The unfathomable.

For me, the absolute worst wasn't just a possibility. It was the expectation.

And now it could cost me Remi.

Every single one of my calls went to her voice mail, which skyrocketed my anxiety.

With my heart in my throat, I paced my living room, loud waves of thunder rattling the windows as I tried and failed to slow my racing heart and mind.

She'd be there soon.

She'd laugh at me for worrying and then willingly dive into my shaking arms.

She wouldn't know why I was losing my mind, but she wouldn't ask questions or pass judgment.

She'd just be there.

Alive. Breathing. Smiling. *Remi.*

At six o'clock, I couldn't take it anymore. I taped a note to my front door for her to call me ASAP and then set out on an all-too-familiar and terrifying search of the city.

White-knuckled and through a torrential downpour, I drove straight to her house, hoping and praying she'd gotten off early, taken a nap, and just overslept. No one was there, not even a car in the driveway.

Her office was locked up tight.

I used her website to find the house listed with the home theater, but she wasn't there, either.

With every dead end, it became harder and harder to breathe. The past triggered memories I'd kept buried deep in my subconscious. So deep that it was the only way I survived at all.

By the time I looped back around to her house, there was a Lexus in the driveway. I didn't want to be this guy. The boyfriend showing up all wild-eyed and panicked, freaking everyone else out too, but fuck, it was almost seven.

My lungs burned as I pounded on her front door. I was soaking wet, but I could have been on fire and still would have preferred it to the unknown swirling in my chest.

Aaron slowly cracked the door, his angry confusion turning to recognition the second he laid eyes on me. "What the hell, Bowen?"

"Where is she?" I rasped, barely able to form words at all.

His chin jerked to the side as he swung the door open completely. "What do you mean where is she? I assumed she was with you."

"Well, she's not." I stabbed a hand into the top of my hair. "She was supposed to be at my house at three, but she's not answering her phone. She's not at the office. She was showing some guy houses today and now it's radio silence."

He shook his head as though he were trying to rattle into place all the puzzle pieces I'd thrown at him. "No. We talked at lunch. She finished with that guy early."

That was but one horrific scenario I could cross off my brain's mile-long list of impending catastrophes. "Then where the fuck is she?"

"I…" he stammered, but I didn't let him finish.

"Call Mark," I ordered. "See if she's with him. Maybe her dad. Fuck, anyone."

He blinked at me, my palpable fears quickly transferring to him. "Wait." His face lit, and he snapped twice, immediately turning on a toe. He marched through the living room and snagged his cell off the coffee table. "I can track her phone. She's good about checking in before and after she meets a new client, but we set it up when she started showing houses alone again."

Oxygen exploded in my lungs, a rush of hope viciously colliding with the adrenaline in my veins. With long strides, I sidled up beside him, both of our gazes aimed at the screen.

And then time stopped.

My heart too.

My lungs seized.

And I choked on the bitter acid of my reality.

"She's at the hospital," he whispered.

Every muscle in my body flexed painfully, and then all at once, I exploded out the door.

The hospital. The fucking hospital. What the fuck was I supposed to do with that? It was still pouring. Had she been in a wreck? Was she hurt? Was she…alive?

I couldn't lose her.

I wouldn't survive this again.

One tragedy after another. For once in my Goddamn life, something had to give.

After climbing into my truck, I slammed the door, the pain in my chest so familiar it felt as though I'd time-traveled into the past. How many times would I be forced to go through this hell before the universe finally decided it had taken enough of my flesh? Fuck, what if it took her? What if that was the end game? Over and over, I would be forced for all of eternity to lose the woman I loved.

I was vaguely aware of Aaron climbing into the seat beside me, but I was a goner, buried six feet deep in the what-ifs.

The pressure in my head threatened to split me in half as I blew every single red light on the way there.

She had to be okay.

There was no other option.

As I weaved through traffic, squinting to see through the rain, Aaron was on the phone with the hospital.

What a fucking shit skill set to have, but I knew all too well how searching for a missing person worked. They asked her name. Her description. Then put him on hold for what felt like a decade.

And then, just fucking like the first time I'd lived through hell, they had no answers. Remi wasn't in their system, and no Jane Does had been brought in, either.

But she was there. Or at least her phone was. And within fifteen minutes, that was exactly where I was too.

I had no idea what I would find as I threw my truck into park at the curb in front of the emergency room. Truthfully, I didn't even know if I'd find her at all.

But no matter how many times my world was rocked, my heart was shattered, or the cruel universe tried to ruin me, for Remi, I would spend the rest of my life desperate and determined to keep her, no matter the cost.

chapter
TWENTY-ONE

Remi

"I CAN'T BELIEVE I LET THIS HAPPEN," TIM SAID WITH TEARS IN HIS eyes.

I gave his shoulder a squeeze. "This isn't your fault. That nurse never should have left her alone."

He let out a humorless laugh. "Are you kidding? Knowing Katherine, she probably told her to go. She's so damn independent, but no matter how many times I try to remind her that she's not Superwoman, I can't slow her down." He closed his eyes, helplessness etched on his round face. "That woman is my entire life, but until the settlement check comes in, I have to keep working and sometimes that requires me to be on the road." His lids fluttered open, a single tear rolling down his cheek. "I don't have a choice but to rely on nurses, and this is the shit that happens."

"Hey," I soothed, dragging him into a hug. "Don't be so hard on yourself. You're an amazing husband. Working to keep the bills paid doesn't change that. Look, she's okay. It's just a broken arm."

"This time," he scoffed, releasing me before blowing out a hard breath. "I don't know how to thank you for being with her today. I have no idea what I would have done without you."

I smiled. "No thanks necessary. She's my friend." I poked a finger in his chest. "And you, just so you know, aren't Superman, either. I'm happy to help, both of you, in any way I can. If you go on the road again, you call me."

"Remi," he whispered. "I can't ask you to do that."

"You can. *And you will*. We're in this together, Tim. I may not have known you guys before the crash, but we're family now. Family leans on family. End of story."

Tears once again filled his eyes. "Thank you. You have no idea how much—"

That was all he got out before a commotion came from the other side of the doors to the waiting area. The sound alone was startling, but my back shot straight when I recognized the two syllables of my own name.

"What the hell?" I mumbled.

Oh, but I knew that voice, raw and jagged as it might have been. My throat got thick, and with hurried steps, I left Tim in the hallway and pushed through the doors to the waiting area.

Bowen was at the reception desk, his white T-shirt soaked and clinging to his muscular back, his hands balled into fists at his sides. Aaron was beside him, his jaw twitching at the hinges.

"Hey!" I called, jogging over. "What's going on?"

"Fuck," Aaron rumbled, pulling me into a hard hug. "Jesus, Remi. What the hell? Are you all right?"

"I'm fine." I looked at Bowen, but he just stood there,

the difference between **SOMEBODY** and **SOMEONE**

staring at me like he'd seen a ghost. His face was the perfect picture of desolation.

"Where have you been?" Aaron snapped as he released me, giving my shoulders a firm shake.

I kept my gaze locked with Bowen's, my mind swirling as I tried to figure out why there was a dark void in his honey-brown eyes, and answered my best friend. "Katherine fell out of her wheelchair. Tim was working a few hours away, so he called me to go over there. I followed the ambulance here and waited for him to arrive. I was just about to leave. What…are you two doing here?"

"Looking for you. You weren't answering your phone, so this guy showed up at the house, losing his mind. And then I lost my shit when I tracked your phone only to find out you were at the hospital." Aaron dragged me in for another hug, but I was limp in his arms.

All of my attention was focused on the man I barely recognized who still hadn't moved an inch, and as far as I could tell he hadn't so much as blinked, either.

I shook my head, stepping out of Aaron's embrace. "I left my phone in the car." Reaching out, I hooked my fingers with Bowen's. The tremble in his hand was as alarming as it was heartbreaking.

Suffocating devastation rolled off him. I could barely breathe as I moved in closer. On the outside, he was cold—emotionless, even—but as I rested my hand over his heart, it slammed violently against my palm.

"Are you okay?"

As if he needed to truly consider the question, he slanted

his head, his first voluntary movement since he'd seen me. "I don't know," he rasped, but even that was strangled.

He gave my fingers a sudden tug, pulling me off-balance and crashing me into his chest, his wet shirt soaking the front of my pale-pink dress. A rumble filled with agony escaped his throat as his arms folded around me so tightly that it was almost painful. I didn't complain though as he buried his face in the curve of my neck, his shoulders hunched, cocooning me as if he were trying to absorb me.

"Jesus, Remi," he choked out. Yes. *Choked*. My strong, stoic man crumbled right in front of me.

Why? I wasn't sure yet, but it was a punch to the gut all the same.

After wiggling my arms from between us, I wrapped them around him, the muscles on his back taut and straining. "It's okay. I'm fine. Everything's fine." I glanced around the waiting room.

Tim and Aaron had formed a huddle off to the side, but all eyes were aimed at us. Bowen didn't strike me as a particularly proud man, but whatever was going on inside him didn't need to be witnessed by a room full of strangers.

"Come on. Let's get out of here." I looked at Aaron. "Did you drive here?"

He shook his head. "I rode with him."

"Good. Then take my car back to the house. I'm going home with Bowen."

Aaron swallowed hard and then nodded, the turmoil of the day showing in the lines on his forehead.

"Hey, I'm really sorry," I told him. "I should have called. I wasn't thinking."

He offered me a tight smile. "Just take care of him. I'm good."

I gave Bowen a squeeze. "Let's go home, baby."

He groaned again, reluctantly releasing me, and I paused long enough to dig my keys from my pocket and toss them to Aaron. He insisted on following us out to make sure I got my phone from my car before we left.

Bowen was still quiet and robotic, refusing to release my hand, so I offered to drive his truck. The scowl and side-eye he gave me were my only real hope that he was going to be okay.

As we drove back to his place, I felt like a total asshole. My guilt magnified when I saw the dozens of missed calls and texts from him. When I'd gotten to Katherine's house and found her on the floor, her arm clutched to her chest, calling to tell Bowen I was going to be late was the last thing on my mind. Naïve as it was, I'd never considered he would be so worried. I also hadn't realized it was as late as it was, either.

In hindsight, it was dumb. Epically so. But I was trying to do the right thing. Katherine was hurt and scared. I hadn't wanted to leave her alone.

However, after I'd seen the terror carved into Bowen's handsome face, knowing I'd put it there shattered me in so many ways. Though, if I were being honest, it confused the hell out of me too. Aaron had been visually shaken, but Bowen's reaction was a different story altogether. He just shut down, leaving behind a husk of the man I knew.

I'd seen him frustrated and annoyed. Hell, I'd even seen him angry when I'd first started pursuing him. But I'd never seen him like this.

The way he shook.

The desperation with which he clung to me.

The hollowness in his eyes alone was a physical blow.

I could only assume it had something to do with his past. Most definitely related to losing his fiancée. But I still didn't know the specifics of that to figure out what had triggered him or why he'd reacted so strongly to me being a few hours late. A few hours in the middle of the afternoon no less. Maybe if it had been three a.m. and I'd disappeared on the way home, but it was barely seven. I'd been tied up at work later than that before.

None of that excused me from fault though.

The rain was still coming down in sheets, so when we pulled into his driveway, he hit the remote for his garage door on the visor and we went straight in. He turned the truck off, clicked the button to close the garage behind us, and unbuckled his seat belt, but that was the only move he made to get out.

The silence was killing me. Every instinct I had told me to fill it with profuse apologies, but they weren't what Bowen needed. Still, I had no idea what he did need, and I had a sneaking suspicion he didn't even know himself.

All I could do was sit beside him, my hand in his, waiting for him to figure it out.

He blankly stared at the windshield, his chest rising and falling with labored breaths for so long that the light in his garage clicked off, plunging us into darkness.

Only then did he speak.

"I thought I lost you," he confessed so softly that it was barely audible.

In the dark, I could only make out his silhouette and wished like hell I could get a better read on him. Bringing our joined hands to my lips, I inched as close as the damn center console would allow. "God. I am so sorry. You're not going to lose me. I swear."

"I did though," he said, his voice filled with gravel.

"No, you didn't." Fuck the console. I climbed over it, wedging myself in the small space in front of him to straddle his lap. "I'm right here, Bowen." I took his hand and rested it over my heart. "Do you feel that? I'm right here. I'm not going anywhere. This is where I belong."

"It could all go away," he said in the dark, the tone in his voice a dangerous combination of fear and anguish but mostly dread.

Helplessly, I sat there, not knowing what to say to comfort him, to make him believe that, although what he was feeling was real, the panic and the tragedy he was living—or, rather, reliving—wasn't. And before I could come up with something, he continued, still without moving an inch or reacting to me the way he always did.

"I don't know if I'll survive all this again. I don't know if I can make it out on the other side if you ever—"

"Shhh," I interrupted before he could spiral even farther down into the abyss. "Don't. Don't do that." I cupped his cheeks, noticing that my hands were now shaking too. "Can you do something for me? Right now?"

Seeming to almost snap out of the anxiety attack that was gripping him like a vise, just to possibly help me, he immediately answered, "Anything, babe."

His breathing hadn't quite regulated, still jilted and uneven. So that was where I'd start. Replacing my hand, I paired my cheek with his so that we were at one another's ear.

My chest against his, I slipped my arms around his back and quietly said, "Breathe with me."

His pulse raced against me.

Nervous sweat coated his skin.

His strong body trembled in my embrace.

"Please. Let's do it together," I whispered against his jaw. "Deep breath in." I inhaled, and he tried to do the same. Although his was shaky and not nearly as deep. But he was doing it.

Only thirty minutes ago, the man in my arms had been ready to burn the world down because he hadn't been able to find me. I could certainly walk through the flames with him to the other side.

"Good. Now let it go. Breathe out."

Had I known that the feeling of his exhale was going to caress my ear and my neck the way it did, I might have thought better of being so close. Nevertheless, I'd have to put a pin in the erotic sensations Bowen gave me—at least until he was feeling better.

"Again, in."

We inhaled. Leather and wet man filled my nose, which probably didn't sound very intoxicating, but the buzz I caught wasn't imaginary.

"And out."

After a few minutes, I quit talking altogether, my mouth having dried from the exercise and the attraction that was building inside me. Soon, we fell into perfect sync.

Our shoulders rose and fell in time. Like two ships swaying on a gentle tide, peace began to wash over the man in my arms. I could feel it. Sense it. The energy in the cab of his truck

the difference between SOMEBODY and SOMEONE

had changed from palpable, crippling tension to one of calmness and unity.

When his hands finally tangled with the hair at my nape, I praised, "There you are." With my chin perched on his shoulder, it was easy for him to steer my face to his. "Did my *someone* come back to me?"

I thought I'd lost him again when he briefly startled at my words.

"What? Didn't think I could find you?" I asked, trying to make light of the milk cartons he surely would have had my face on by morning. It wasn't the time for jokes though.

"I didn't know you were looking," he rasped.

"Always." As I adjusted myself to get a better glimpse of his face in the almost pitch-black, I felt something very serious between us.

"You *are* mine, Remi," he stated as if the whole damn world were listening. "I need you right the fuck now."

Like a period to the intense and heavy moment we'd just shared, the mood shifted. I was all too ready. Too eager to give him whatever he wanted. Whenever he wanted it. Even if that meant drenched in the front seat of his truck when there was a perfectly good king-sized bed only a few dozen feet away.

Turned on by his declaration and hunger for me, I rolled my hips.

Sucking air through his teeth, he palmed my ass and pulled me so close I couldn't tell who the throbbing at our centers was coming from, but it was most likely a combination of both of us.

"Now's good," I agreed, breathless.

In a swift move, he leaned me back as far as I could go against the steering wheel, but when it wasn't far enough for him, his hand left my breast and adjusted the power seat, giving us all the room we'd need.

"Front or back, Remi?" he asked.

Confused, I answered, "I-I've never done that, but if you're—"

A wicked chuckle rumbled through the cab. "I mean, how does your dress open? Buttons in the front or zipper in the back?"

"Oh. The zipper."

"Okay. But I like where your head is at, Ms. Grey. Not tonight though. I need something more rough right now, and I'll want to take my time with that."

I swallowed. It was a lot of sexual information all at once, and considering how my mind was already in a torrent of wanton desire, I was going to let that one go and think about it later.

I didn't want to miss a thing.

Because at that point, he'd already spun me around on his lap, unzipped my dress, pulled it over my head, and tossed it to the passenger seat.

I wasn't sure how he'd managed, but when he leaned forward to press kisses across my shoulder blades, he was shirtless too—and making short work of ditching his pants underneath me.

"I'll buy you new panties. Now, hold on to the wheel for me."

Trying to remember how, just minutes ago, I knew how to breathe well enough to instruct it, I recalled the process, but it was much more like panting than I'd care to admit.

I gripped the wheel as he'd told me while he ripped first the right, then the left side of my thong. Wasting no time, two long fingers raced over my crack and headed straight to my wet center.

"Fuck," he growled. "Already so wet."

I wasn't sure if he would see my face, but I looked over my shoulder and said, "Don't you know by now that I want you just as bad as you want me, Bowen? Maybe more."

"Goddammit," he swore. "Fucking hold on."

He entered me with such force that I cried out, half pain, all pleasure. He held himself deep inside me and pulled me even closer by the hips, thrusting as if there were any more ground to gain.

"Are you ready?" he asked. If I hadn't known in my heart that he'd never hurt me, he would have sounded ominous and almost frightening. But I'd never been turned on as much as I was in that moment.

"All of it," I answered.

Unmerciful.

Unrelenting.

Unencumbered.

Unyielding.

Every strike found my core. Every thrust, I met him for another.

After he masterfully found my clit, lit a fuse, and waited for me to go off on his cock and his hand, he growled, "All fucking mine," through what sounded like clenched teeth as he came.

We sat there for several moments, his fingertips biting into my hips, the sound of our labored breathing filling the truck. Reaching around, he palmed my breasts and eased my upper body back to rest against his chest. The scruff on his jaw tickled my shoulder.

"If I tell you I love you now, I risk it coming off as a product of desperation. If I don't, I'm a lying fool."

I smiled, my stomach dipping in the best possible way. Putting my chin to my shoulder, I peered back at him. "Then I won't tell you I love you too and we'll be even."

He blew out a ragged breath and kissed my shoulder.

Hitting the light above the rearview mirror, I blinded us both. When I was finally able to see again, I glanced around the truck, my clothes strewn everywhere. "You know I haven't had car sex since—"

"Ever," he finished. "My cock is still inside you, babe. The answer is you haven't had car sex ever."

I giggled. "Well, obviously, that's what I was going to say."

"Perfect," he rumbled, giving me a tight hug.

"Hey, Bowen?"

"Right here."

"You know we're going to have to talk about earlier, right?"

He drew in a deep breath and then held it for several seconds. "Yeah, I know. Let's get you inside and cleaned up first."

chapter
TWENTY-TWO

Remi

"Rᴇᴍɪ," Bᴏᴡᴇɴ ᴄᴀʟʟᴇᴅ ꜰʀᴏᴍ ʜɪs ʙᴇᴅʀᴏᴏᴍ, ʜɪs ʙᴀʀᴇ ꜰᴇᴇᴛ padding toward me. "What are you doing? I thought you were getting some water."

I lifted the full glass in his direction but continued to stare down at the crack at the bottom of his guest room door, two little black paws sticking out.

We still hadn't had our talk. When we'd come in from the garage, he'd joined me in the shower, his hands washing every inch of my body, including my hair. It wasn't sexual, but it was intimate all the same.

I returned the favor, lathering his chest with soap while peppering kisses across his collarbone. Every so often, my name would flow from his lips on a pained whisper, but he never followed it up with anything more, so each time, I simply replied with a reassuring, "I'm right here."

We once again skipped his elusive burgers, opting for a

pizza I'd found in his freezer. Side by side on the stools at his bar, we split a bottle of wine, and even as we ate and drank our dinner, his hand never left my thigh. The wine lightened the mood a fraction. He'd managed a smile when I'd pinched his ass, and a few minutes after I'd pulled on one of his T-shirts to sleep in, he'd waggled his eyebrows, following it up with an ass grab of his own.

As I stood in the hall staring down at his pup's feet under the door, he walked up behind me, pressing his front to my back, and slid his arms around my waist. "He's not stuck. He's at the door because he can hear you out here."

"He is kinda stuck though. They sleep in your room when I'm not here, right?" I couldn't see his face, but he kissed the top of my head.

"They're fine, babe. I took them outside while you were brushing your teeth. Gave them both treats. Even fluffed their dog beds. Not that Sugar will use his, but I put extra pillows on the guest bed for his majesty."

The little feet shuffled from under the door, and guilt slashed through me. "First, I stole their dad, then their bed. My future step-dogs are going to hate me."

Bowen's chest shook with a chuckle. "Those two aren't capable of hating anyone. One piece of lunch meat and all grievances are forgiven."

Like he was suddenly fluent in English, Sugar let out the cutest bark, going crazy as if he could dig his way out.

Bowen had been great about keeping them put away while I was at his house, but if I was to be a permanent fixture in his life the way I so hoped, I would have to get used to them sooner

the difference between **SOMEBODY** and **SOMEONE**

rather than later. "Do you think I could meet the little one? Maybe ease into things?"

Bowen slid around in front of me. A grin twitched his lips. "Now?"

"Yeah. Why not? Poor guy obviously isn't ready for bed yet."

His mouth stretched into a full-blown smile. "You sure? He's a wild child. But he won't hurt you. He'll jump on you. Tap-dance. Cover you with kisses, maybe even sneak a few on your lips if you aren't careful, but I swear to you he's the sweetest dog you'll ever meet."

"I believe you, but can we maybe do the lunch meat thing too? Just in case he's holding a grudge about the recent sleeping arrangements."

He laughed, but the happiness sparkling in his eyes made me feel even worse for not doing it earlier.

"Be right back." In less than a minute, he returned from the kitchen with two slices of ham.

Of course he'd brought two.

Bowen was a good dog daddy. He wouldn't dare deny Clyde a snack if Sugar was getting one.

He handed me the meat wrapped in a paper towel. Nerves almost two decades old churned in my stomach as he cracked the door. I waited for Clyde to plow over his owner, trampling Sugar in his herculean wake. But Bowen simply scooped Sugar up with one swift movement, tucking him under his arm, and then calmly ordered, "Stay."

Chancing a peek into the room, I saw the mammoth dog sitting in the middle of a huge, round dog bed, the tip of his tail thumping the wood floor. Terrifying as my brain thought the brown beast might have been, he was also pretty damn cute with his droopy jowls and floppy ears. Bowen tore off a piece of the meat before walking over and offering it to him. I waited for my man to pull back a bloody stump, but Clyde was a gentleman, sniffing it before delicately taking the ham between his teeth.

"He was hoping for cheese," Bowen said, ruffling his ears.

"Right, so I'll bring a block of cheddar when I'm ready to meet him."

He laughed and headed back my way. Luckily, Clyde made no move to bolt out the door and maul me. With all of my limbs still intact, I'd already chalked the doggy meet and greet up as a huge success and I hadn't even officially met Sugar yet.

"Easy, boy," Bowen mumbled. His fingers tangled with mine as he led me to the bedroom.

Sugar wiggled in his grip, locking eyes with me over his shoulder. It was probably because he smelled the ham, but I pretended he was just excited to meet me—and not at all kill me in my sleep.

"All right," Bowen said as I got comfortable on the bed. "Here's how this is going to work. Tear off a little piece of the ham and I'll set him down. Fair warning, he's going to do exactly two zoomies around the bed before stopping for the treat. Then he will immediately do another two."

I crinkled my nose. "Zoomies?"

"Race around in laps. It's his nightly ritual. Don't fight it. When he's done, he'll want the rest of the ham. If you aren't quick enough, he'll bark. But that's all. I swear to you he's a lover, not a fighter, and I'll be right here with you the whole time."

The dog couldn't have weighed more than five to ten pounds. I felt relatively confident I could handle my own if he

the difference between SOMEBODY and SOMEONE

turned rabid. But it was sweet how patient and reassuring Bowen was with me. Come on. I was a twenty-nine-year-old woman scared of a poodle. It wasn't my most attractive trait.

"You ready?" he asked.

I tore a corner of the ham and blew out an even exhale. "As I'll ever be."

He set the dog on the bed, and I waited for the so-called zoomies. Instead, Sugar pranced over to me, bypassing the ham I was all but trying to shove down his throat, and climbed up my chest, licking my face any and everywhere he could reach.

Bowen had been right. He definitely caught me on the lips a few times.

"Are you good?" Bowen asked, studying me intently.

"Yep." I giggled, pushing the dog out of my face. He collapsed into a ball on my lap, rolling in every which direction, his nubby tail wagging a mile a minute.

Bowen sank beside me on the bed and gave the dog's belly a rub. "See? I told you he wouldn't hate you."

I laughed as Sugar jumped right back up, catching me with a kiss on the chin, before taking off in a dead sprint around the bed. He came to a sliding stop in front of me, letting out a loud yip that made me jump, but after a quick nibble of ham, he was back off to the races.

"Is he always this hyper?" I asked as Bowen leaned back against the headboard, kicking his legs out. Sugar did not hesitate to launch himself over them mid-dash.

"He's actually calmed down since we got him."

It was strange. I knew Bowen had a whole traumatic history involving his lost fiancée. It had never even occurred to me to be bothered or jealous by a woman who had lost her life.

But there was something about the way he'd said *we* that hit me squarely in the chest.

I tried my best not to let him see it, but I must not have been quick enough to hide the flinch. He took the paper towel from my hand, gave the last treat to Sugar, and then put his arm down around my shoulders, dragging me against his side, resting my head on his bare chest.

"Ah, shit, I fucked that up," he groaned.

"No, you didn't," I lied.

Sugar trotted over to us, staring for a minute before climbing up Bowen's body like a billy goat. He circled three times, looking for the most comfortable place on his human, then flopped down into the curve where my stomach met his dad's side, half on, half off both of us. I gently stroked his back while listening to the slow and steady rhythm of Bowen's heart.

"You can ask, ya know?" he finally said.

I tipped my head back to look at him. "I don't want to ask. I want it to be something you share. Something you trust me with. A relationship is give and take, Bowen. This isn't something I get to take from you with questions."

"Jesus," he breathed, threading his fingers through the top of my hair.

"You don't have to tell me at all. But I can't read minds, and I can't stop things from hurting you if I don't know what they are. I messed up tonight. I'm more than willing to admit it. But you scared me too. Something awful happened inside you, and it's killing me to think I could unknowingly cause that again."

"It's not your fault," he said adamantly. "Please, God, never say that any of this shit is your fault. It's just..." His Adam's apple bobbed, and he shook his head. "When I met Sally, it was a whirlwind. Time wasn't a factor. In the span of three weeks, I'd fallen in love and planned a future." His gaze collided with mine. "When I know, *I know*, Remi. It's how I feel when I'm with you."

I melted into his side. Funny enough, I understood completely. From the moment I'd laid eyes on him at the courthouse, I'd had no doubt he was *someone* special. I didn't know how or why or when. But I always felt the unexplainable connection when we were together.

"I feel it with you too."

"Good." He kissed my forehead before continuing. "A week shy of our one-month anniversary, I got drunk and ballsy and asked her to move in with me. She'd thought of every reason in the book why it was too fast, but she never said no. The next morning, she disappeared."

My body jerked as puzzle pieces from that afternoon started snapping into place. Shit. It hadn't been about the plane crash at all.

He paused only long enough to draw me tighter against his side. I got the feeling it was an attempt to ground us both, and dread pooled in my stomach.

"I called the few friends of hers I knew at that point. They hadn't seen her, so they turned around and called her family. No one knew where she'd gone though. Her car, her purse, her cell phone, and several suitcases of clothing were missing. The cops were notified but told us there was nothing they could do about a woman going on vacation. And by all accounts, that was honestly how it looked. But my instincts wouldn't shake the feeling that something had happened to her. I felt it in my bones. The worst part was, once I explained that I'd asked her to move in with me, everyone, even her family, started to believe the cops too. They thought I'd spooked her. Too much. Too soon." He let out a low growl. "Not my Sally though."

I'd said I wouldn't ask questions. I'd sworn to myself I was just going to let his thoughts flow and accept whatever parts of himself he wanted to reveal. But my heart was in my throat, suddenly frozen in fear of where the story was headed. "Wh-what happened to her?"

"That's the one question that ruined us all. Five days later, they found her in her car at the park where she'd said she was going for a run. I'd searched every inch of that trail at least a dozen times before that and there was no sign of her or her car, but somehow, she miraculously just showed up one day, drugged out of her mind."

A chill pebbled my skin. "What?"

"She wasn't into drugs. Her friends said they'd dabbled with stuff in college, but when they found her unconscious, there were needles and heroin beside her, track marks on her arms. Everyone was so quick to assume she'd gone off on some kind of bender. The police, the doctors… Hell, even her best friend bought into it for a while. Everything was a haze for her, but she was adamant that a man had kidnapped her and given her the drugs against her will."

"Holy shit," I breathed. It wasn't the most eloquent or supportive response, but what the hell else was there to say?

"Yeah," he muttered. "It was awful. She was hysterical, but she had so few memories of what had happened to her over those five days that we couldn't make the cops do anything. They dusted her car for prints, but that was about it. They told us just to be happy they didn't arrest her," he scoffed, but even that sounded pained. "I was so fucking relieved when they found

the difference between SOMEBODY and SOMEONE

her. She was alive, and that was all I needed. But little did I know it was only the start of the hardest chapter of my entire life."

My eyes closed, a sick unease swelling in my stomach. What in the world could have possibly made it worse?

"She wasn't the same woman when she came home, Remi. And who could blame her? She'd survived hell. But where she'd once been so fiercely independent, she became terrified of everything. And when she wasn't scared, she was obsessing about another woman who she swore had been kidnapped too and held in the same cold, dark room with her. She didn't know anything about her or what she looked like, but her cries haunted Sally's dreams. She spent entire days camped out at the police station, begging them to find her. But once again, without anything to go on, the police wrote her off. And they weren't the only ones. She and her best friend had a falling out over her inability to let it go and focus on her own recovery. Her dad tried to convince her to start therapy, but he made the mistake of sending her to a facility that included an inpatient drug program, which promptly sent her over the edge."

Unshed emotion sparkled in his eyes. "And there I was, stuck in the middle, desperately holding on to mere pieces of a woman I would have given anything to put back together, without the first clue how to help her."

"Oh, God, Bowen." I curled my hand around the side of his neck.

Sugar was having none of Bowen getting all the attention, so he army-crawled up, hitting me with a drive-by kiss to the nose on his way, and curled up like a cat on his dad's shoulder.

An almost genuine smile tipped the side of Bowen's mouth.

And in that moment, I was more grateful than ever for the needy dog.

He gave the pup's head a scratch. "Not too long after that, I gave her Sugar, naïvely hoping he would be a distraction. Sally was timid with Clyde at first too, but they became fast friends, and I thought having her own dog that could go back and forth between her place and mine would be good."

Leaning his head to the side, he gave Sugar a snuggle. "She was so damn happy those first few weeks. Doting on him. Babying him. Buying him outfits. I honestly thought she was coming back to me. But it was all a ruse. She figured out the only thing I needed to be happy was for her to smile. And fuck me, she played the part like there was an Oscar up for grabs. None of it was real though. She was still scared. Broken. Shattered. Consumed by guilt and pain." His gaze came back to me, his smile sinking into a sea of regret and shame. "She tried to kill herself three separate times."

My whole body seized, and I bit my lower lip. Tears rolled down my cheeks. Who I was crying for, I couldn't be certain. My heart ached for Bowen and everything he'd been through, but dear God, that poor woman.

"Hey," Bowen whispered. "Please. Don't cry."

My shoulders shook with a sob. It was official. I was the world's worst support system. I was supposed to be comforting him, yet my whole body trembled and my lungs burned for air that couldn't quite make it past the boulder on my chest. "It's a lot, Bowen. For both of you. I can't even imagine…"

"And you'll never have to." In one swift movement, he plucked the dog from his shoulder, set him on the floor, and then rolled into me. His front became flush with mine, nose to nose, his minty breath whispering across my skin. "I would give up my entire life to make sure you never have to imagine a single second of that, Remi." With soft, gentle kisses, he dried the tears from my cheeks, taking my pain as his own as if his wasn't enough.

Gliding my fingers into the back of his hair, I murmured against his lips, "Did they ever find the man who took her?"

"No."

"The other woman?"

He leaned away far enough to catch my eye. "No."

A wave of grief crashed down over me, stealing my breath. Empathy had always been my strong suit, but this felt as though I'd been caught in the undertow. "Oh, God."

His arms tightened around me. "Don't do that. It broke her. Don't put this on your conscience too."

I sucked in a shaky breath, willing my racing mind to slow. There I was, lost in anguish over a story, when the man I was falling in love with had lived every horrific detail.

Jesus, Remi. Get it together. This isn't about you.

But in a way, it was.

"I am *so* sorry about not letting you know where I was. You must have been terrified."

His arms sagged the smallest fraction, and he blew out a breath. "I was. I thought it was happening again. And when I realized you were at the hospital, it hit me like a brick wall that, even if I found you physically, it still might not be *you* who came home with me."

"Oh, Bowen." I buried my face in the curve of his neck. "It's still me. I'm right here. I swear."

"I know. It's just going to take a while for it to really sink in. For me to believe it's real."

"Well, I'm here for as long as it takes."

He stroked the back of my hair. "That might be forever."

"Okay. I kinda like it here."

He let out a low hum. "You think I'm kidding."

"I hope you're not."

His arms cinched around me, and he turned his face to kiss my cheek. "There you go again, making it impossible for me not to say I love you."

"You don't need to. I think I got a head start on falling in love with you anyway."

He stared at me for a second, his warmth encompassing me as his gaze branded me more than any declaration of love ever could. "Don't be so sure about that."

And then he kissed me.

Deep and hungry.

Carnal and consuming.

His lips were a promise.

My moans were a plea.

And as he tore the T-shirt over my head and drove inside me, our bodies joining as one, I was positive there was no more falling left to be done for either of us.

chapter
TWENTY-THREE

Remi

Me: My Uber took the slowest route possible. I'm so sorry I'm late.

Bowen: Babe, it's 6:01. Late for you doesn't start until at least 6:15.

After the incident at the hospital, I'd spent the next week being the world's most punctual and communicative girlfriend. I'd texted Bowen every morning when I woke up. He'd laughed because five of those times he'd been lying in the bed beside me. I'd also texted him before showing houses, after showing houses, and during lunch, and again, two of those times he had been sitting across the table from me.

He'd never asked for any of it. It wasn't a trust or control thing. But if it made him feel comfortable to know where I was, a simple text was the least I could do.

It wasn't like I was alone in the understanding and thoughtful department. While Sugar and I had officially become besties, Clyde still scared the shit out of me if we ran into each other when he was loose in the house. Bowen—my sweet, sweet Bowen—had tied a bell to the collar of his hulking, one-hundred-plus-pound goodest boy so he could never sneak up on me. Give and take. It was all about the give and take.

Me: Okay, well, anywho, I'm walking in now, Sirfriend.

I flashed my ID to the bouncer at the door and then walked into the crowded bar. It was trivia night, and since I hadn't been in a few weeks, I was far past due to thrash some drunk co-eds who thought they knew it all. And to ensure my victory, on this particular night, I'd brought a secret weapon.

Not so shockingly, he'd been early. It wouldn't have been Bowen if he hadn't. But as I caught sight of him at a small hightop table wearing a tailored suit, complete with a vest that honestly might have been hotter than the sleeve-rolling thing, I regretted being even a few minutes late.

He stood as I approached, immediately pulling me into a hug.

"You look dashing," I said.

He traced a hand down my side, stopping to tease the exposed flesh where my pink T-shirt failed to meet my short denim cutoffs. "You should have told me it was a college bar. I would have gone home to change first."

I leaned away and smiled. "Oh, please. You look amazing. Plus, now everyone will think you're a professor and be on their best behavior."

His eyes darkened and he slid his hand down to my ass,

the difference between SOMEBODY and SOMEONE

slipping it into my back pocket before giving it a firm squeeze. "Well, in that case. Miss Grey, I graded your essay today and you failed miserably. I will be offering extra credit tonight, but it will involve an oral presentation."

My entire body heated, not at all limited to my cheeks. Using the lapels on his jacket, I dragged his mouth down to mine, kissing him indecently—or at least it was indecent for two people in or nearing their dreaded thirties like ourselves. "You're so gracious, Professor Michaels. I assure you my presentation tonight will be my finest work to date." Hopeful and horny, I slipped my hand inside his jacket and... Bingo. I pulled out a clean, neatly folded handkerchief. "Perfect, I needed a good luck charm." I shoved it down the front of my shirt and into my bra for no particular reason other than I liked the idea of him spending the night thinking about my boobs. "However, until we get home, I need to borrow your brain and not your body."

He let out a deep rumble, and as I'd hoped, he glanced around to see if anyone was watching before sneaking his fingertips under the hem of my shirt, trying to get his hanky back.

I did not miss the way his fingertips slid across the curve of my breast.

And he did not miss my soft moan or the way I licked my lips.

"Fuck," he rumbled. "What's the prize for winning this little trivia thing?"

"Little?" I scoffed, using his wrist to remove his hand. "I think not. There are two orders of nachos and a pitcher of beer up for grabs here."

He arched an eyebrow. "Import?"

"Domestic, but whatever. A win's a win."

"Orrr...I buy you nachos and a beer that is actually palatable and then we both win-win naked back at my house and skip the whole damn thing. What do you say?"

I patted his chest. "Nice try. But I have a good feeling about tonight. I've never won before. Aaron is terrible at trivia. Smart guy, but he's about as speedy at picking answers as a ninety-year-old man with no hands."

"What makes you think I'm any faster?"

Pressing up onto my toes, I nipped at his earlobe. "Those fingers gave me two orgasms the other night. You help me win this, I'll let you try for three."

I started to move away, but he caught the back of my head, holding me a breath away from his mouth. "You are an evil, brilliant woman. But as soon as this is over, you get a raincheck for your nachos and beer because I'm claiming number one on the way home." He licked the tip of his finger before tracing it over my bottom lip.

My breath caught. *Damn.* Suddenly, I'd never wanted to play trivia less. But I'd committed, and honestly, getting off on Bowen's fingers as he drove me home was a much better prize than nachos.

"Okay, then," I whispered. "I guess I'll...go get us signed up."

He smirked as he let me go, but it morphed into a full-blown laugh as I reached into my shirt, pulled his handkerchief out, and dabbed it across my flushed face as I headed to the bar.

I'd been wrong. Bowen wasn't good at trivia. The man was freaking *incredible.*

The bar issued everyone an electronic device and then questions appeared based on the designated category. Each question was multiple choice, A through F. Some had more than one answer and you had to pick all of them to be right. Others had no correct answer at all, so you had a button for that too. Points were assigned based on how quickly you submitted the correct answers, and I was not wrong about Bowen's long, dexterous, and nimble fingers.

He dominated every history, sports, and math question to appear on the screens mounted around the bar. I pulled up the rear with pop culture, literature, and geography.

The only reason it wasn't a complete blowout was the damn science category. We struggled through though and managed to have a ninety-nine-point lead over Team Beer Goggles by the end of the third round. The only problem was the final question was worth exactly one hundred points, and I didn't need Bowen to do any accounting to know that if we got it wrong, we would end up in second place with nothing more than the order of cheese sticks as a consolation prize. I loved a good mozzarella stick as much as the next girl, but dammit, Team Sexy Professor was no loser.

After a few taunting glares at the Georgia Tech frat boys across the bar, Bowen and I huddled together, shoulder to shoulder, the rectangle touchscreen centered on the table between us and our eyes glued to the TV in the corner.

What 1989 film directed by Rob Reiner follows two fated lovers for over a decade as they attempt to settle the debate of whether men and women can ever truly be strictly platonic friends?

I hadn't finished reading the question before I stabbed my

finger down on the screen so fast I nearly elbowed Bowen off his stool.

I didn't bother to look to make sure we'd gotten it right. I could have done a one-woman play reenacting that movie word for word if they'd asked for it.

"Yeah, buddy! Take that!" I shouted, launching myself into Bowen's open arms.

Stools tipped. Drinks sloshed. He spun me in a circle, laughing, not a lick of good sportsmanship to be found in either of us. In fact, I think there were a few boos from the other teams, but whatever. I had just won nachos and orgasms. I was allowed to celebrate.

Out of breath but still laughing, Bowen and I sat down and waited for the waitress to bring our gift cards to claim the future spoils of our victory.

"Holy shit, Remi. That was amazing. You were an animal," Bowen teased. "I barely saw Rob Reiner before you had already answered."

"Damn right." I brushed invisible lint off my shoulder. "Though I'm not sure I would have been that fast with any other film. I have a slight obsession with *When Harry Met Sally*. I've watched it no less than two hundred times."

He shook his head. "No way. That movie is older than you are."

"No, seriously. My freshman year of college, the TV I had was a crap hand-me-down, and by second semester, it wouldn't change channels anymore, so I was stuck at the mercy of the TV gods for what I got to watch. I swear, for a month straight, *When Harry Met Sally* came on every day. I hated it at first, but it was background noise while I studied, and eventually, I'd memorized the entire thing. When my TV finally died, I missed it." Smiling, I leaned in close. "Harry Burns especially. The way that man used humor to hide his sadness pulled every single one of my heart strings. Anyway…I bought the DVD and the movie became the soundtrack of my college years. You ever seen it?"

"Actually, yeah. Although Billy Crystal didn't do anything to my heart strings."

I laughed. "Well, it's clear whoever created the questions tonight has never seen it. Harry and Sally weren't fated lovers. They were friends who fell in love. Thus proving the debate that men and women *can't* just stay friends." I slanted my head and thought about Mark and Aaron. "Present company excluded."

Bowen propped his elbow on the table and lifted a finger. "Wait, wait, wait. You don't think they were fated lovers?"

"Psh, no. They had to grow on each other. She hated him at first." I pursed my lips and tapped them with my fingertip. "Sounds like somebody else we know, huh?"

"I never hated you, and she didn't hate him, either." He rolled his eyes. "Oh, come on. That car ride, where her friend just so happens to set them up on an eighteen-hour road trip together when they'd never even met before? The airport? The bookstore? There is no way all of that happened by coincidence."

I crossed my arms over my chest and stared at him. "Holy hell, Bowen Michaels. This might be more surprising than the truck. Do you believe in fate?"

He nodded, firm and confident. "Absolutely I do."

"What? How?"

"What do you mean how? Fate is about predestination and the development of events beyond a person's control." His handsome face was so serious that I didn't want to laugh at him. But I was barely holding it back.

"So let me get this straight. You believe your entire life has already been determined. If that's the case, what's the point in living?"

"Just because there's a path doesn't mean you have to walk it. Was I destined to be an accountant? I don't know. I'm happy though. In some other life, could I have been more successful in a different career? Possibly. I guess what I'm saying is this goes back to the whole *somebody versus someone* thing. Somebody is a person you found. Someone is a person fate picked for you. Let me guess, you don't believe in soul mates, either?"

My jaw fell open. No way. Of all people. After everything he'd been through, there was no way this levelheaded, pragmatic man was about to tell me he believed in *soul mates* too. And not because I thought the entire idea was beyond ludicrous—which I did—but mainly because he had been *engaged* before. Planned a life with a woman. Was going to spend *forever* with a woman. Did that make Sally his soul mate? Shit. That was even her name. *Sally.*

More so, if Sally was his soul mate, then what did that make me?

Mozzarella sticks.

A ball of fire formed in my chest. What the hell was my problem? Why did I keep getting hit by a wave of jealousy every time we talked about his ex? The woman wasn't even alive. How could I possibly be bitter that he'd once been in love with her?

Oh, right. Because I was in love with him now. In the present. And the mere idea that I didn't have all of him was a dagger in my heart.

the difference between SOMEBODY and SOMEONE

It should be known that green was not my color.

Exhibit A: "So do you think the plane crash was fated?" I snapped.

I shouldn't have asked it. It was childish, spoken out of some seriously misplaced resentment. And the guilt when he flinched was more painful than any therapy I'd done since the crash itself.

I slapped a hand over my face as if I could hide. "Don't answer that. Oh, God, do *not* answer that. I am a horrible human being. You officially get to keep both the nachos. I'll upgrade the pitcher of beer for you too. Fuck, what is wrong with me tonight?"

He tugged at my wrist, trying to pry my hands away. "Babe, stop. It's okay."

"No, it's not. That was a really shitty thing to say."

The legs of his stool scraped across the floor, and I felt his thighs close in around the outside of mine. With his hand on the back of my head, he guided my forehead to rest on his shoulder. It was a half-assed barstool hug—and still more than I deserved.

"It wasn't shitty. You asked it with a shitty attitude for some reason, but the question itself is valid."

"I never should have—"

"Hey," he whispered in my ear. "I wouldn't wish that nightmare on anyone, but I absolutely believe fate was in control of that flight. At least for me. Because through a statistically impossible chain of events, it brought me here. With you."

Oh my God.

Oh.

My.

God.

While I was having some sort of jealousy-induced stroke, comparing myself to a deep-fried appetizer, this gorgeous and wonderful man was sitting beside me, thinking fate had brought us together.

Chancing a glance at him, I tilted my head up. "I wish it hadn't taken a plane crash for us to meet."

He smiled and used both hands to palm my face. "Me too. But fate isn't always the good stuff, Remi. Sometimes the path provided isn't a straight line but rather a journey filled with obstacles and detours. It took the unimaginable for me to find you, but I will never stop being grateful that there was even one single junction in time in which our paths crossed."

I closed my eyes and blew out a shaky breath. I was grateful for that too. Whether it was fated or coincidence didn't matter. Bowen Michaels was mine.

I wanted to tell him I loved him.

I wanted to tell him I was sorry he'd lost Sally.

I wanted to tell him that, whether I believed in soul mates or not, I knew that he was someone I saw a future with.

But I'd said enough for one evening. "Let's go home. It's getting late and three is going to take you a long time."

He grinned. "And you have an oral presentation to prepare for."

I brushed my nose against his. "After that win, your fingers have done a lot for me already tonight. What do you say you give them a rest and we both do a little oral presenting… at the same time?"

I don't know how it happened, but in the very next blink, I was off my stool, one of his arms under my legs, the other wrapped around my back to hold me against his chest.

"Bowen!" I laughed, clinging to his neck.

"You better get your nachos," he said, carrying me past our waitress.

She lifted a paper gift card in the air, and I snagged it from her hand as he paraded me out the door as if I were the real prize he'd gone there for.

Turned out, Bowen's fingers didn't need a night off after all.

He made me come with his hand down the front of my shorts on the way home.

On his mouth, atop his couch as soon as we walked through the door, unable to even make it to the bedroom.

And just before midnight, he finished the hat trick with his cock, me on my knees, him taking me from behind.

chapter
TWENTY-FOUR

Bowen

"Soooo, how's work?" my mom asked through the phone as I wiped my bathroom counter.

I rolled my eyes knowing good and damn well this call had absolutely nothing to do with my job. We'd been on the phone long enough for me to scrub down both the bathrooms, sweep the kitchen, fold a load of laundry, and pack up another load to be dropped off at the dry cleaner.

Tyson gave me hell for not hiring someone to clean for me, but there was something therapeutic about the act of such mundane tasks. Maybe it was the distraction of it all, or possibly the ability to wash the past away and start fresh and new. But whatever the case might have been, it afforded me countless hours to humor my mother and sister with their marathon phone calls.

"It's good. Oscar is finally moving into his office next week. When I named it Michaels & Company, I had no idea the company part would be so hard to find. But it will be nice not to have to turn away business for a change."

"Anything else going on in your life that you might feel the need to tell your mom about?"

There it was: the real reason she called.

With the phone wedged between my shoulder and ear, I rinsed the rag out. "You mean like something Cassidy may have told you, but I haven't yet, so you called and talked my ear off for over an hour until you eventually ran out of things to say so now you're passive-aggressively asking since I still haven't spilled the goods?"

"Sure," she chirped, no shame in her game. "You got anything like that you want to tell me? I'm really more like a friend, you know."

Grinning, I tossed the dirty cloth into the bucket and flipped the light off. "Hardly and not really."

"Bowen Alexander Michaels," she scolded. "Why are you torturing me with this?"

I barked a laugh. "I'm not torturing you. I'm happy, Mom. How much more do you need?"

"Oh, I don't know. A name, birthdate, and social security number should be plenty."

My mom was wild in the best possible way. "You are not running a background check on my girlfriend."

She gasped, and if I knew her at all, tears were already forming in her eyes. "Your *girlfriend*?"

"Well, technically, she likes to be called Madame Mouthy but yes. Same thing. It's still new, but she's incredible, so I didn't waste any time making my move."

"Oh, honey," she breathed, but it did nothing to hide her

pure joy—or relief. "I... You... This is...wonderful. Just absolutely fantastic news."

"Are you crying?"

"I'm your mother. Of course I'm crying."

"I thought you were more of a friend."

"As your friend, shut up when your mother is crying."

Sugar barked when there was a sudden knock at my door. Remi wasn't supposed to be there for at least another hour, but maybe hell had frozen over and she was early for a change.

"Mom, I gotta go. Someone's at my door."

"Don't you dare drop this on me and run. I need details. What's her damn name? Where's she work? What's her shirt size?"

I pulled the phone away from my ear and stared at it as though she could get the full force of my side-eye. "What the hell does it matter what size shirt she wears?"

"Christmas will be here before you know it. She can't be the only one showing up at the family Christmas party without a personalized sweater. She'd be embarrassed!"

"Trust me. Firsthand experience says she is gonna be more embarrassed if you make her wear one of those holiday travesties. It's not even summer yet. Relax. You've got time."

The knock came again. This time, it was so hard it rattled the windows on the front of the house.

"I'll fill you in later. It's not imperative that the entire Michaels family run her off already."

"Bowen!"

"Love you, but I gotta go!" I hung up before she could interrogate me further—and before whoever the hell was at my door could break the son of a bitch down.

the difference between SOMEBODY and SOMEONE

Just as my hand landed on the knob, there was another loud pounding.

"What the hell?" I rumbled, snatching it open.

There was no time to even register who was on the other side before pain exploded at my cheek. I stumbled, my shoulder hitting the wall beside the door to keep my balance.

Through my dizziness, I was able to make out Aaron's voice as he yelled, "What the fuck, Mark!"

Ah, yes. *Mark.* Suddenly, all the who, what, and whys made a lot more sense.

"What the hell did you do!" he roared, his hand wrapping around my throat as he pinned me to the wall.

I was a big guy, tall with lean muscles, but Mark was like an NFL linebacker. Regardless, none of that stopped me from rearing back and cracking him in the jaw.

"Motherfucker!" he boomed, never releasing me.

Well, not until Clyde finally responded to Sugar's yaps and came barreling down the hall, his teeth bared, a deep, malevolent bark echoing through the living room. Even amongst the chaos, I found it interesting that my old pooch was a protector after all.

"Clyde!" I called, not wanting to add a dog attack to this clusterfuck. "Sit."

He slowed to a jog, still growling at Mark as he parked his ass beside my foot.

Mark had the good sense to shove off me, and Aaron quickly slid between us with his arms stretched wide to separate me from him.

"Can we all just calm down?" Aaron snapped.

"You son of a bitch," Mark seethed around his buddy. "What the fuck is going through your head right now? Please.

Just make this make sense. What? Your dick got hard, and suddenly that's all that fucking matters?"

My blood boiled. "You better watch your fucking mouth. It's nothing like that, and you know it."

"I don't know shit anymore." Murder showing on his face, he dove back at me.

I easily dodged him, but Clyde jumped on his hind legs and snapped at his hand. In desperate need of space to ensure Mark left with all of his appendages, I grabbed Clyde's collar and walked him to the back door. Sugar all too happily trotted out behind him.

I slammed it shut and planted my hands on my hips before giving the asshole my attention back. "Would you fucking relax?" I flashed Aaron a glare. "Great job keeping your mouth shut."

"Oh, don't you dare pin this on me. I didn't say a damn word. She hasn't been home in a week. What the hell did you expect?"

Mark laughed without humor. "You better start talking fast. I have never in all my life wanted to kill a man more. You gave me your word. You gave *all* of us your word."

"And I kept my word!" I roared, my patience snapping. "Even when it fucking corroded me from the inside out, I kept my head down and let her live her life. But this wasn't my choice. She came to me. She was relentless." My chest heaving, I let six months of agony spill from my lips. "Seeing her at the courthouse nearly destroyed me. But I did it. I walked away. Just like I promised. But then, at McMurphy's, she appeared out of nowhere, slid right up beside me, talking a mile a minute. I tried so Goddamn hard to run her off. Honest to God, I was burning at the stake each time her eyes dimmed. But still, I kept my word because that was what was best for *her*."

"And yet here we are, with her sharing your bed."

"What the hell did you expect me to do? You know Remi. There is no stopping her once she sets her mind to something. She showed up at my office, all lovestruck and starry-eyed." I dug my wallet out of my back pocket, fished out the safety pin, and held it in the air. "She gave this back to me. You can't possibly look me in the eye and tell me that doesn't mean something?"

Aaron swallowed hard and cut his gaze to the floor. It was obviously not the first time he'd heard this story.

Mark's chin jerked to the side, his mouth a hard slash. "Are you… Are you saying she remembers?"

My stomach knotted. The burning ashes of all the hope I'd been carrying since she'd waltzed back into my life rained down over me, searing my skin. "No. There's nothing there. For fuck's sake, she brought me peanut butter cookies. But she's drawn to me in ways she can't explain." I swallowed past the razor blades in my throat. "Look, after the plane crash, when we realized she'd lost her memory, I promised I would stay away as long as she didn't remember. But she's in there. She's not the same Sally I fell in love with, but for fuck's sake, she's still in love with me."

Mark's jaw ticked at the hinges. "You selfish bastard. You're gonna ruin her life. We hit the fucking lottery when she lost that year of her memories. We got her back, and you're going to throw that away over some ridiculous notion of love? Do you even fucking remember how bad it got after she disappeared?"

My hand flexed at my side, fighting the urge to bury it in his face again. "I don't need a refresher course. I was there every

Goddamn agonizing day. I still can't look at my hands without seeing them covered in her blood."

"If she remembers, we all risk losing her again."

He wasn't saying anything I hadn't already considered. After Remi had given me the safety pin back, I'd spent the entire night pacing my house and berating myself for even considering letting her back into my life. The whole reason I'd agreed to walk away to begin with was because I didn't exist in the version of her life she remembered after the plane crash. And neither did the five horrific days when she'd been kidnapped. She wasn't haunted by fear or trauma. She wasn't angry because the authorities didn't believe her. Nor was she overwhelmed with guilt for not being able to save the woman crying in the corner. It was as if her brain had rebooted, deleting the timeline in which the world had broken her.

The doctors had told us talking about the time she'd lost and showing her pictures might help jog her memory.

But all we'd wanted was for her to forget. *Permanently.*

It was all too easy to remove me from her life. She had decades of memories with Mark, Aaron, and her dad before the plane crash. There were only three weeks with me that weren't tangled up in the horror of the week she'd been taken.

Everything about us had been wrapped in tragedy.

The fear was that my presence would trigger something in her brain.

And when I saw her smiling outside that hospital, and I mean, really smiling—like the Sally I'd fallen in love with damn near the minute I'd laid eyes on her—I knew that was not a chance I could take.

During the depths of her darkness, I told her there was

the difference between SOMEBODY and SOMEONE

absolutely nothing I wouldn't do to take the pain away. As it turned out, that included letting her go.

But knowing she was out there, happy and healthy, breathing easy, surrounded by people who loved her—that was all I'd needed. I never stopped loving her though. Never stopped wishing she'd come back to me. It was wholly selfish, yet I still dreamed.

But what if we could have it all now?

She didn't remember our inside jokes, late-night soul-baring conversations, or even how I'd proposed. Sally, the woman I had spent nine months falling in love with, was gone. But Remi was very much alive and well. She didn't have to remember. She was already on the verge of falling for me again. Maybe this was the miracle we'd all been praying for.

Mark and Aaron might not have agreed with what I was doing, but I didn't give the first fuck what they thought. They'd gotten to keep her. They hadn't spent the last six months with a gaping hole in their chest, struggling for one single breath that actually contained oxygen. Fuck them and anyone else who thought they could stand in my way.

The world owes you nothing.

But somehow, it had still given her back to me.

chapter
TWENTY-FIVE

Bowen

Nine months before the plane crash...

"Thanks, but I'm good," she said from the end of the bar, shooting down her fifth man for the evening.

Not that I had been keeping count. Or watching her—intently—in the mirror behind the bar for the last hour. Thank fuck for the TV screen mounted on the wall or I would have looked like the creep I so clearly was.

"You sure?" Baldy Can't Take a Hint asked.

Lifting the full appletini she'd been nursing since she sat down, she smiled, and to her credit, it at least appeared genuine. "I'm all set, but I appreciate the offer."

I cringed, embarrassed for the poor schlub as he started to sit down on the stool beside her. He could have stood there all night and she wouldn't have asked him to leave. But this, I'd learned, she would shut down quick.

the difference between SOMEBODY and SOMEONE

Extending her hand over the stool, she stopped him. "Actually, I'm expecting someone."

"Oh," he said, sounding surprised.

Come on, dude.

She was fucking stunning. Sexy, long blond hair. Blue eyes that could bring a man to his knees. Long black dress with thin straps that exposed enough cleavage to be mouth-watering but still keep my mind racing for what else was hiding beneath.

Of course she was expecting someone. Women like that didn't just sit at a bar alone, waiting for the first chump to ask to buy her a drink.

My whole body jerked when her gaze suddenly flicked up, colliding with mine in the mirror. As much as self-preservation told me not to, I held it for a beat, unable to look away. She was smiling, but that wasn't new just because her eyes were aimed at me. Still, it felt like I'd been slapped by a heat wave.

She turned her attention back to the guy. "Yeah. Sorry."

"No biggy." He shrugged, his ego visibly deflated. "Have a good night."

"You too," she chirped.

Defeated, he walked away like the parade of men before him.

And just like with all the others, my lips twitched with a grin.

I should have left over an hour ago. Technically, I'd asked for my check before the blond goddess had walked in. One glance and I wasn't going anywhere. Until I figured out who she was waiting for—a friend or the luckiest bastard in existence— my ass was glued to that stool.

Staring blankly at the sports highlight reel on TV, I turned my glass of whiskey in my fingers.

"All right," she said from an alarmingly close proximity.

I swung my head to the side and found her sitting next to me. Like, right fucking next to me, her soft floral scent filling my senses.

"You're gonna play the strong, silent type. Don't worry. I like it." She smiled. Bright. White. Life-altering.

Fuck me, she was even more beautiful up close.

"Are you waiting on someone?" she asked. "Friend? Wife? Girlfriend?" She paused and slanted her head. "Boyfriend?"

My gaze dipped to her lips. "None of the above. But I thought *you* were expecting someone."

"Well, I was. Then I realized he would rather eye-fuck me in the mirror than come over and start a conversation."

Busted. And I couldn't even be mad about it.

"You're not nearly as sneaky as you think you are." She lifted her martini glass for a sip, and when she put it down, it was almost empty. She must have thrown it back before walking over. Probably a little liquid courage. And fucking hell, wasn't that a confidence booster.

"You're sitting here, so I guess it worked." I winked.

She clinked the rim of her glass with mine. "Touché. Maybe you're a genius after all."

Probably not a genius, but I was smart enough to know she needed another drink. My small talk was not sharp enough to keep her entertained for long. I lifted my chin at the bartender, and he immediately came walking over.

"Can I get an appletini?" I asked.

the difference between SOMEBODY and SOMEONE

He nodded and wandered away. Just another day at work for him.

"So, do you come here often?" I asked her. No, seriously. That was what I said. See the aforementioned part about my small talk.

"Nope," she replied, popping the P. "I was showing a condo down by that new plant shop. I happened to see you through the window on the way to my car. Figured a drink couldn't hurt."

My brows shot up. "Oh, so *you* were actually the creeper in this scenario?"

"Guilty." She lifted one shoulder. "Honestly, I had no choice though. A gorgeous man in a dress shirt with the sleeves rolled up? I'm surprised I didn't have to wait in line."

"Says the woman who slayed the hearts of half the men in this bar."

Confident and brazen, she beamed at me. "All but the one I wanted."

Fucking fuck me. Pink cheeks, full lips. Damn, she was gorgeous.

"Then the sleeves did their job."

She giggled and shook her head just as the bartender set the appletini down in front of me.

"You want to open your tab again?" he asked.

"Yeah," I replied, never tearing my eyes off her.

She leaned toward me, resting her foot on the bottom rung of my stool. "From whiskey to appletini. That's an interesting… and appalling transition."

Shaking my head, I slid the drink her way. "It's for you."

"Ohhh," she breathed, resting a hand over her heart. "That's sweet. But seriously gross."

"Wait. Isn't that what you were drinking?"

"Not even close." She pushed the drink away. "I'm usually a wine girl, but they're out of the New Zealand Sav Blanc tonight so I had to make do. Cosmo, hold the cranberry, because ew. Replace it with sweet-and-sour mix, which I would like to note they do not make from scratch here. And instead of an orange twist, I asked for a lime."

My head snapped back. "What in Sally Albright hell kind of drink order is that?"

Her eyes flared comically wide, and her jaw slacked open. "What did you say?"

I waved her off. "She's a character from—"

"*When Harry Met Sally*," we said in unison.

She stared at me as though she had a front-row seat to a bigfoot spotting. "No way. No freaking way." She narrowed her eyes. "Where did they first meet before driving to New York?"

I grinned. Finally, growing up being tortured by my older sister was paying off for me. "Chicago."

"The orgasm?"

"Katz's Deli."

She drew in a sharp breath, her breasts stretching the limits of her dress. "Too much pepper?"

"Paprikash."

"Oh my God!" She slapped a hand over her mouth.

I turned on the stool, and my knees brushed hers. Quite proud of myself, I leaned in close and lowered my voice. "Did I pass?"

Suddenly, she stood, her stool nearly falling over behind her. "I need to leave."

My arrogance fizzled. "What? Why?"

"Because I'm twenty-eight," she announced as if it answered all of life's great questions.

Twisting my lips, I replied, "And I'm thirty-one."

"Fuck." She stood up and snatched her purse off the bar. After fishing her hand around inside, she pulled a few bills out and threw them onto the counter.

I quickly collected them and tried to hand them back to her, but she was a woman on the run. And there was not one damn thing that could have stopped me from chasing her.

"Hey, wait!" I called, clueless as to what the hell I could have possibly said wrong. I'd quoted an old movie, not confessed to being an axe murderer.

She made it just outside the pub door before I caught her.

Careful not to touch her, I tucked the cash into the top of her purse and then I stepped in front of her. "Wait. Don't go."

She shook her head. "Look, I'm sorry. I'm not ready to get married yet."

My back shot straight. "Who the hell proposed?"

"Don't give me that," she sighed. "Those eyes, that shirt, questionable taste in drinks aside, you know *When Harry Met Sally*. I am practically three-quarters of the way pregnant with a house in the suburbs and I don't even know your name."

"It's Bowen, and as much as I am not suggesting a pregnancy in any way, the last quarter you're missing is by far the most fun part of the process."

She tilted her head back and stared up at the night sky. "Oh, God, you're clever too? It's going to be twins. I'm too young for this."

I chuckled, and unable to stop myself, I rested a hand on her hip. "Don't go. I can't do much about the eyes, but I promise to roll down the sleeves and put the kibosh on all further conversations about Meg Ryan movies."

She swayed forward, resting her hand on my chest. I prayed like hell she couldn't feel my heart trying to escape my rib cage. "It's not going to be enough. I don't know how, but I knew you were going to be trouble before I even walked into the bar. I was kinda hoping you'd prove me wrong and be completely obnoxious."

I bent at the knees, bringing us eye to eye. "There's still time, ya know? I have this horrible habit of interrupting people and a peanut allergy that makes eating out super frustrating. Trust me, an hour with me, and I might—"

I stopped midsentence as her breast quite literally sprang from her dress as the thinnest of straps snapped.

"Noooooo!" she gasped, slapping a hand over her black lacy bra.

I tried to be a gentleman and not look, but for fuck's sake, I was no hero.

"This fucking dress," she seethed, crossing her arms over her chest, her broken strap dangling over her shoulder. "I swear it's cursed. As soon as I get home, I'm soaking it in gasoline and burning it to ensure the safety of mankind."

Fuck. She was funny too, and if I didn't act fast, I was going to lose her.

Frantic, I glanced around without the first clue how I was going to salvage the moment. She already wanted to leave, and with her dress now broken, I didn't have much of a shot at convincing her to stay. But nothing was impossible, and when it came to this woman, even if it was, I'd try anyway.

"Do you believe in fate?" I asked, moving into her space.

the difference between SOMEBODY and SOMEONE

Tilting her head back, she peered up at me. "Not particularly."

"Okay, well, I do. So hear me out." I brushed her blond hair off her shoulder, my fingertips grazing her soft skin. "What if it's not cursed? What if it's actually your good luck dress?"

She let out a loud laugh, but she didn't back away, so I chanced hooking my finger with hers. She not only allowed it, she turned her hand so her fingers braided with mine.

Fuck. Yes.

Okay, breathe.

Do not blow this. Do not fucking blow this.

"I've never been to this bar before. You said you hadn't, either. Atlanta's a big city. What are the chances that we'd both just happen to end up here tonight? And before you read into this, I'm not proposing or asking you to fall in love with me and especially not asking you to bear my children. But what if we were supposed to meet?" I squeezed her hand. "Don't go. Let me buy you a drink and get to know you."

She shook her head. "In case you didn't notice, I'm having a slight wardrobe malfunction at the moment."

Victory sang in my veins. That wasn't a no.

"Okay. Then what if we let fate decide?" I pointed at the door. "If I can find a safety pin in there to fix your dress, you'll stay and give me a chance. If not, I'll walk you to your car and let you go...*after* you've given me your number and agree to go out with me tomorrow night."

She narrowed her eyes. "Why do I feel like those odds are stacked in your favor?"

I shrugged. "I don't make the rules, Sally."

Her mouth tipped into a lopsided smile. "Well, then, who would I be to deny fate?"

A huge smile split my lips. I didn't care if I had to origami a safety pin out of a fork. I wasn't letting that woman go. "Excellent."

Holding her hand, I led her back into the bar, my gaze flashing around, ready to ask every patron in that place if I had to.

Oh, but fate had better plans for me.

The hostess smiled at us. I was fairly certain staring at another woman's chest while holding hands with someone else was never a good idea, but a silver glint where a button should have been caught my eye.

"Wait here," I told my *date* before heading to the hostess.

"Hi," she greeted. "You guys want a table or are you heading back to the bar?"

"I need that safety pin."

Her chin jerked to the side. "What?"

"The one on your shirt, where your button is missing. I need it."

She laughed uncomfortably. "Um, sorry." She used her hand to cover the front of her shirt. "I'm kinda using it myself right now."

I could have stood there all damn night and waxed poetic about *When Harry Met Sally* and predetermined destiny. But I was already wasting time.

I pulled out every bill I had, quickly counting them. "I'll give you two hundred and sixty-six dollars for the pin."

She blinked rapidly. "Are you serious?"

"Completely."

the difference between SOMEBODY and SOMEONE

"I, um..." She swallowed hard. "I'll get fired for flashing the customers without it."

I let out a low growl and glanced over my shoulder. Sally was watching me, a humor-filled expression on her face. It only made me want to kiss her that much more.

"Fine." I immediately started unbuttoning my shirt. "Two hundred and sixty-six dollars and a shirt."

"Deal." She laughed, snatching the cash from my hand.

Luckily, I was wearing a white, fitted crew-neck undershirt, but I was not above sitting at the bar shirtless if that was what it would take.

The hostess handed me the pin and then disappeared with my shirt into the back, presumably to change, while I sauntered, smiling like a maniac, back to my Sally.

Bending at the waist, I presented her with the pin. "Madame."

"I'm not sure we can consider that fate as much as bribery. But you made your point." She took it from my hand and pulled the two pieces of fabric together to temporarily fix the dress. It wasn't perfect, me in my undershirt and her being held together by the grace of God and a one-inch pin, but somehow, it was better.

"You gonna tell me your name now?" I prompted, offering her my elbow.

She slid her arm through mine. "Remi. But I kinda like it when you call me Sally."

The story continues in
The Difference Between Somehow and Someway

other BOOKS

From the Embers

Release

Reclaim

THE RETRIEVAL DUET

Retrieval

Transfer

GUARDIAN PROTECTION SERIES

Singe

Thrive

THE FALL UP SERIES

The Fall Up

The Spiral Down

THE DARKEST SUNRISE SERIES

The Darkest Sunrise

The Brightest Sunset

Across the Horizon

The Truth Duet

The Truth About Lies
The Trust About Us

The Regret Duet

Written with Regret
Written with You

The Wrecked and Ruined Series

Changing Course
Stolen Course
Broken Course
Among the Echoes

On the Ropes

Fighting Silence
Fighting Shadows
Fighting Solutude

Co-Written Romantic Comedy
When the Walls Come Down
When the Time is Right

about the
AUTHOR

Originally from Savannah, Georgia, *USA Today* bestselling author Aly Martinez now lives in South Carolina with her four hilarious children.

Never one to take herself too seriously, she enjoys movies that can surprise her with a twist, charcuterie boards, and her mildly neurotic golden retriever. It should be known, however, that she hates pizza and ice cream, almost as much as writing her bio in the third person.

She passes what little free time she has reading anything and everything she can get her hands on, preferably with a glass of wine by her side.

Facebook: www.facebook.com/AuthorAlyMartinez

Facebook Group: www.facebook.com/groups/TheWinery

Twitter: twitter.com/AlyMartinezAuth

Goodreads: www.goodreads.com/AlyMartinez

www.alymartinez.com

Printed in Great Britain
by Amazon